DRAGON'S LORE

Dragon Guard, Book 39

JULIA MILLS

DRAGON'S LORE

Dragon Guard Series #39
Paladin Warriors - 2

by
Julia Mills

There Are No Coincidences.
The Universe Does Not Make Mistakes.
Fate Will Not Be Denied.

❀ Created with Vellum

ACKNOWLEDGMENTS

Cover by Rebecca Pau with the Final Wrap
Proofread by Tammy Payne with Book Nook Nuts
Formatted by Black Paw Formatting
Golden Czermak with FuriousFotog

DEDICATION

Dare to Dream! Find the Strength to Act! Never Look Back!
Thank you, God.
To my girls, Liz and Em, I Love You. Every day, every way, always.

To Golden, Cover model and Photographer. Like the Hero of this
story, Golden is fearless in the face of adversity, loving to all he meets,
and a true inspiration. ROCK ON, GOLDEN! Love you to the
moon and beyond!

This one's for all the fighters out there. Those of you who've been
knocked down but refused to be beaten. You got back up! Dusted
yourself off! And kept fighting, kept putting one foot in front of the
other! You are a TRUE WARRIOR!
YOU ARE MY HEROES!

INDEX

Index of Ancient Languages
Dragon Kin and Inuit
Dragon's Lore

Gaelic

Mo Chroí..........My Heart
Mo Gráh..........My Love
Rún Naofa..........Sacred Secret
Màthair..........Mother
Sipsach..........Gypsy
A bhobain.......... My Darlin' (or lil' rascal)
Mo Thíogair..........My Tigress

INUIT

Ananaksaq..........Grandmother
Atâta..........Dad
Akuluk..........Sweetheart
Kul..........Darling
Kamiks..........Boots

THE DRAGON GUARD

We soar the skies
Free to a certain extent,
As long as we stay hidden
From prying human eyes.

Our scales differ in color
Our defensive weapons,
Tails, horns, talons and all,
Are never the same.

We are one with nature
We blend in with nature
The wind helps us soar high in the heavens
While the earth grants us healing strength in our hour of
need.

We are one with the world
We are the guardians of our kin
When evil conspires to maim and hurt
We are protectors of this human race.

As majestic animals of fairytales
We share our beings with great men
They walk in honor and the grace of Fate,
Fate that we cannot deny.

CHAPTER ONE

"*L*ore..." *Bang – bangbangbang – BANG* "Lore! LORE!"

Refusing to open her eyes, she gripped the edge of her favorite Sherpa-lined blanket as tight as she could while burying her face deep in the soft down of her pillow. As the door flew open, the resulting whooshing breeze brushed strands of her long dark hair across her face. The smack of the doorknob slamming against the metal plate she'd screwed into the wall rang out like a dinner bell being rung. The stomp of booted feet across the carpets in her room was the completion of the announcement that her roommate had entered the room. Holding on as tight as she possibly could, she couldn't help but smile as the blanket violently jerked in her hand.

"Wait for it," she whisper-giggled to herself. "You know it's coming. She's nothing if not predictable."

"Damn you, Lore!" The threat was low, almost a growl but still human enough that it was apparent Minka had her Leopard under control...*for the moment*. The bed shuddered as the renowned zoologist, and infamous hothead kicked the

1

frame before roaring, "Get your ass outta bed right-this-minute!"

Making a show out of stretching one arm and then the other over her head before rolling over and yawning so wide her jaw literally cracked, Lore gave her furious friend a sleepy smile and mumbled, "Something wrong?"

"Is something *wrong*?" The last word was perfectly, angrily drawn out for dramatic effect. "Did you *really* just ask me if something was wrong?" Doing a precise about-face and marching, not pacing the length of Lore's bed, Minka's hands were going up as high as they possibly could from within the thick arctic-wear parka the zoologist still wore then down, then up, then down, over and over, until she resembled a bundled-up Raven as she railed away. "YES! There's something *fucking* wrong. There's a dead man in our Clinic. Not an animal. Not a bird. Not even a reptile or a fucking fish. A. Man."

Biting the insides of her cheeks to keep from laughing, Lore opened her eyes as wide as they would go and put on her innocent face as her best friend and exploration partner stopped short, spun towards the bed, leaned over, and spat, "A. *Dead*. Man. In. Our. Lab. Why?"

Squirming out from under her blankets and skootching her butt upward across her mattress until her back touched the hand-carved headboard, Lore pushed her long, ebony hair back from her face. Clearing her throat while trying not to smile, she clarified, "Well, (a) I don't *think* he's dead, only frozen and will be revived by his magic because he's a Dragon Shifter. (b) If he is dead, his body has to be returned to his Clan because that's the way of the Dragonkin and we do *not* want to make enemies of those big guys. And (c) Did you see those markings across his chest and down his arms and legs? They are fabulous and not all Dragonkin."

"No, and I..."

"Then, you weren't looking." Tossing off her blankets and throwing her legs over the side of her bed, Lore launched herself off the tall sleigh bed, her maternal great-grandfather had made with his own two hands a hundred years before she was born, onto the floor as she continued to talk over her furious roommate. "That *man*, as you call him, is not only one of the revered Dragons, not only a *Guardsmen*, he's a freakin', honest-to-the-Goddess *Paladin*."

"So?"

"So?" It was Lore's turn to throw her hands in the air as the clueless look on her friend's face once again reminded them how very different their formative years had been. "Are you serious? Did you not pay one frikkin' bit of attention during Shifter History 101?"

"You know damned good and well I didn't have the most 'conventional' upbringing, even for a Snow Leopard raised in the tropics. Mom was a hippie Wiccan, and dad was...well..."

"I know. I know. Germaine was a pot-smokin', ganja-growin' Leopard with dreads." Holding up her hands in surrender, Lore sighed, "Sorry, sorry, sorry. I always forget because you are so fucking smart and have your shit to-*gether*." She gave a single clap to emphasize her point. "It's just hard to imagine your parents smokin' weed and dancin' naked on the beach under the full moon while you were reading Jane Austen and Shakespeare."

"Do *not* remind me," Minka sarcastically snorted. "I work hard to repress those memories." Shivering with disgust, she added, "Naked parents, *ewwwwwwwww*. It's a wonder I'm not in therapy."

With the mood in the room brightening, Lore breathed a sigh of relief. Minka was nothing if not single-minded. To get her to change directions was difficult in the best of circumstances. Only after years and years and years of friendship had

Lore figured out the right combination of levity and fact to get the Leopard out of her own head.

"Therapy is not all it's cracked up to be. Even if I was there as an experiment for my dad."

Chuckling, Minka winked, "I wish your sessions were videotaped. It would've been fun to see firsthand."

"Yeah, it was. Thankfully, the guy was a friend of mom's. Otherwise, I might still be wearing a straitjacket and taking antipsychotics." Laughing along with her friend, Lore took a deep breath and continued, "Well, for those of us forced into tutor-taught classes at the spry young age of three, the Paladins are a group, or in Dragon language, a *Force* within the race itself who were appointed by the Universe Herself to be the long arm of the Law."

"For who?"

Pulling sweatpants over her long johns and topping it with her favorite 'Hiss Off' tiger-cat sweatshirt, Lore put on a second pair of socks before sliding her feet into her fur-lined Adirondack boots as she answered. "For the whole damn Paranormal world, at least, that was their reason for receiving a shitload of extra magic and superhero powers like three-thousand years ago."

"And now?" Minka asked, casually crossing her arms across her chest and leaning against the doorframe with her brows furrowing in her 'this-is-interesting-tell-me-more' expression.

"Well, as each Shifter race became more organized, the Paladins were only called in for the worst cases, the ones that needed unbiased policing by a third party. Then even those instances became few and far between. Alliances were secured, making each race able to solve all their specific issues internally. After that, the running theory was that they were in seclusion because they weren't needed anymore. Which was stupid. Not only are Dragons not the type to hide away, but..."

"But your father had other ideas, and he shared them with you."

Laughing out loud, Lore agreed, "He shared them with anyone who would listen. Argued with more than one person about his beliefs. Never gave up, 'cause that wasn't his style. Dr. Thaddeus Bransfield was never one to hold back or wait for someone to ask what he thought. In his opinion, knowledge was free, to be shared, and a power that all should seek."

"Yes, I remember that from the many heated debates we had on the evolution of the dung beetle."

"And that's the *shit* I try to repress. Dung beetles? It still creeps me out that you studied them for *years*." Rolling her eyes, Lore shot to her feet and headed towards the door. Looking up from her height of five-foot-nothing to her friend's six-foot-one inches, she gave a single nod and a wink before stepping out into the hall and continuing, "Dad believed that the Paladins were sent to find the Berserker Dragons after they mysteriously disappeared. It all fit with the timeline *and*, he had it on great authority, one he wouldn't share with mom or me, that they were tasked by none other than the Celtic Goddess Morrigan to find *her* Warriors. You see, she's the one who gave that specific Force of Dragons their 'special powers.'" Making air quotes mostly to irritate her best friend, she just kept going as Minka groaned and mumbled something suspiciously sounding like, "I freakin' hate that gesture," under her breath. "Somewhere in his research, dad came across an ancient tome of Gaelic writings detailing the orders given to the Commander of the Paladins by the one and only Phantom Queen."

Appearing at her side with a look of pure awe at the same time that Lore opened the five-inch-thick, steel door leading to the steps to their underground Clinic, Minka excitedly asked, "Seriously? You're not fuckin' with me? A written account of Morrigan's orders? And he authenticated these writings? They still exist?"

Nodding as she pushed the door all the way open and crossed the threshold, Lore confirmed, "He did, with the oldest living Dragon Elder on the planet, Carrick."

"Son of a bitch," the Leopard cheered. "Why didn't I know anything about this?" She stopped pouting for a second, adding with a wink, "And I totally dig the way the old guys use only their first names. They're like rock stars. Ya' know, Madonna, Prince, Cher."

"Okay..." She drew out the word, not shocked by her bestie's little trip to La-La Land, but once again amazed at the workings of her manic brain. Getting back to the subject at hand, she added, "My guess? Or are we playing twenty questions?"

"Duh. Yeah. Your guess. I can hardly have a séance to ask your dad." Slamming her hand onto her hip and giving a sassy raise of her shoulder without missing a step, Minka snorted, "And you know how much I *hate* twenty questions."

Shaking her head and rolling her eyes, listening to the sound of their boots striking the metal stairs as they descended, Lore jumped off the last step. Feeling her friend's growing anticipation as she keyed in the access code for their lab, she teased, "I just love that my sarcasm is wearing off on you, but as happy as that makes me, it's also truly annoying." Barking out a laugh, she added with a wink, "However, under my expert tutelage, you are truly excelling."

Waving her hands with impatience, Minka groused, "Just answer the question. You can pat yourself on the back later. Hell, you can even pick on me for the way I eat pizza with a knife and fork, and I won't retaliate."

Stopping short, Lore spun towards her friend, pointed her finger at the tip of Minka's nose, and demanded, "Promise?"

"Yes," Minka loudly groaned.

"Remember, you promised. I'm enacting the RULE. I get five unimpeded minutes of smartassery if I forgo my need to be funny right now."

"Deal. Now, hurry your ass up, or I'm rescinding my offer."

"Okay." Spinning back towards the keypad, she finished the numerical sequence, opened the door, and with a flourishing sweep of her hand, bowed, "After you, Madam."

Following an irritated and muttering Minka into the massive, stainless-steel, custom-built, fully-automated, absolutely incredible, wonderfully scientific environment she'd designed and commissioned with part of her inheritance, Lore smiled wide as the motion-activated lights flickered on.

Walking into her dream come true, a place all her own where she could study the effects of climate change on animals - both Shifter and non-Shifter - north of the sparsely inhabited Nunavut territory always brought a smile to her face. All her life, people, not her parents or her best friend, but others, lots and lots of others, told her she would never be able to stand the harsh weather. Some said she would never get the permits to build her Clinic/lab. Others said she couldn't do it without her parents.

But she'd proved them all wrong. She'd done it.

There was no doubt in her mind that her mom and dad were looking down from the Heavens, pride shining bright in their eyes, cheering her on. She was who she was because of them. Her brains, her tenacity, her sense of humor, her ability to see all sides of whatever was in front of her, and most importantly, her ability to tell people to go straight to Hell with a smile on her face. They'd given that to her, and there was no way she was going to waste it.

Hurrying to explain before Minka's 'crazy Leopard switch' got flipped, she confided, "You were in the middle of your second doctoral thesis, working day and night on the evolutionary patterns of Avian Shifters versus Typical Avian Species, the Paladins and an old book were not something you needed to be bothered with."

"But he knew how much I wanted to talk to Carrick. How much I love history and digging through old texts. That Dragon Elder has more real-life experience in evolution in his pinky finger than all the authors of all the books I've ever read combined."

"Yes, and he knew that your second doctorate was more important because Carrick wasn't going anywhere." Stopping beside the door to the refrigerated unit, she grabbed the handle and looked her friend dead in the eye. "Carrick is my godfather. We can call him anytime."

"I know that, but this is the first time you've said anything about this or mentioned Carrick, and your dad's been gone for eleven years."

Nodding, sure her over-analytical, super-intelligent friend would later make something out of her lack of emotion, Lore shrugged, "I hadn't thought about it until I found this Dragon under a foot of snow and ice." Pulling the vertical metal handle, she added, "Hell, I wouldn't have known he was there if I hadn't been all furry and walkin' on my paws."

"One of the perks of being a three-hundred-pound White Siberian Tigress when the mood strikes," Minka chuckled then quickly added, "Have you called your godfather yet?"

Ignoring her friend's inquiry, Lore snickered, "Sure is and a helluva lot warmer than this short, stubby body."

"Short and stubby?" The Leopard mocked. "What do you weigh? A hundred-and-ten-pounds soaking wet?"

"I'll be takin' the fifth, my...Son of a bitch!"

"What? What's wrong?" Suddenly by her side, Minka echoed Lore's original sentiment with a hushed, "Son of a fucking bitch! How the...? Where - Where is he?"

Picking up the sheet she'd covered him with and looking at the stainless-steel gurney praying he'd magically appear, that she was having a moment of hysterical blindness, or that she'd gone and lost her ever-loving mind, Lore finally spat, "How the hell do I know?" Glaring at her friend, she added, "*You* said he was dead."

CHAPTER TWO

"*M*e?" The statuesque Amazon screeched. "You're the doctor. You should've checked his pulse, or heartbeat, or whatever it is you *people* do to see if your patient's dead or alive. Isn't that part of the hypocritic oath?"

"It's Hippo*cratic,* and I'm a veterinarian, Dumbass," she deadpanned. "He's a man, not a dog."

"What's the difference?"

Rolling her eyes while ignoring her friend's rude comment, the dark-haired veterinarian continued, "I told *you* I was pretty sure he was only frozen." Stomping her foot as she closed the distance to her friend before pushing up onto her tippy toes, she growled through gritted teeth, "And since *you* were the last one in here, and *obviously* left the door unlocked, *you* get to turn all furry and use that big nose of yours to sniff him out."

"Why me? You brought *it* home. Shouldn't you be cleaning up after it?"

"He's. Not. An. *It*." She shook with frustration, the air

around her crackling like an open power line with unspent magic and a plethora of irritation.

"Well, he's not completely a man either," the tall one grumbled as a new kind of mysticism filled the room accompanied with the scent of freshly fallen snow and blustery winter winds a split-second before she transformed into a large, sleek, spotted Snow Leopard.

Lifting her head, the black rosettes a stark contrast to their white background, she clamped her long, sharp canines onto the edge of the sheet covered in his scent, she pulled the material to the floor before making a show of snuffling and growling while side-eyeing the shorter woman. Much to his chagrin, but not surprising in the slightest based on the enchantment flowing from her Big Cat, it was only a matter of seconds before her light gray nose was pointed downwards, looking for his trail.

Wrapped in the magic of his Dragon, blending into the granite as if he were a chameleon, it took copious amounts of what little energy he could summon to not only hide his person and his scent but to simply stay upright. Scooting away from the Leopard's impeccable sense of smell, the Dragon was forced to bite his tongue to keep from crying out as searing pain wracked his battered body. Like a voracious colony of fire ants biting and gnawing with vengeful aggression, his nerve-endings caught fire as they flipped back and forth between thawing and healing. Only the constant stream of ancient enchantment flowing from the Tigress kept him from falling face first onto the floor and slipping back into a coma.

Was she even aware she was healing him? Forcing her magic through the tiny bond she'd opened within his damaged soul? Could she feel their connection? Had she come to him on purpose? Was she really looking for him? Did she need to save him? Or was everything just another useless, pile of steaming bullshit in a long line of useless, piles of steaming bullshit shit that paved his ironically maniacal tale of tragedy.

The real question was, did it matter? There he was. Another pit he'd have to climb out of. Another mess to clean up. But still, she was nothing short of incredible.

Strength and power filled her aura. Pulsing with untapped energy, she was a force completely unto herself. Unabashed in her behavior, direct and outspoken, so intelligent her mind was a constant stream of thoughts and ideas. She was larger than life. He'd known from the first moment her soul touched his. She was his miracle.

How her five-foot frame contained all the energy, creativity, and raw magic was unfathomable. Uniquely exquisite adhered his mind for it was the perfect description of the amazing woman.

In human form, she couldn't have weigh more than a hundred-and-ten pounds, dressed in the heaviest Arctic gear around. But as her Tigress, she was no less than three-hundred-and-fifty-pounds of fierce predator. The contrast was as stark and awe-inspiring as her heterochromatic eyes.

Drifting in and out of consciousness, trying to force himself to heal and escape where she'd left him before she returned, he'd dreamt of looking into her one light blue and one brown eye. Had *known* her long, ebony hair would feel like silk sliding through his fingers. And did not doubt that her small, taut curves would fit perfectly against his much more significant, steely body. But they were dreams, wishes really, the only thing he'd ever have, *ever achieve*, was the life of a man driven mad.

His fate sealed at thirteen years of age. Damaged beyond repair. Body broken. Mind mangled. Spirit shattered. There was no way he would saddle someone as beautiful as the woman before him with the utter wreck of a man he was.

Sliding one foot to the side and then the other, staying a few feet ahead of the Leopard, his body shook. As the broken, scarred, and mutilated skin of his back scraped against the stone walls, he revisited the sensual tingle from the feel of the soft fur of her Tigress. He vividly remembered how it cradled his frozen body and healed his broken spirit while she carried him across the icy tundra and into the steep and craggy mountain. She was not only his savior or his Guardian Angel; she was also his Mate. For him, there could be no other.

"Dammit, Lore," the Leopard's snarl traveled the telepathic airwaves, crashing through his mind like the ocean's angry waves against the shores of his childhood home. *"His scent is fucking everywhere. What did you do, drag him from one end of this place to the other?"*

"Yeah, Minka," the Tigress sassed her answer. "That's exactly what I did. He was frozen, frostbitten, frail, bruised, and battered... for all intents and purposes, dead, but I rolled him all over the floor for the shits and giggles of it."

Whipping her huge spotted head to the side, the Leopard bared her teeth and hissed before intuitively growling, *"Yes or no. That was all I needed. Not a snark-ass dissertation on the way you treat your patients."*

Slamming her clenched fist onto her hip, the woman he now knew as Lore, leaned down until her eyes met the Leopard's and growled right back, "No. Better?" Extending her hand, she flipped the tip of the Leopard's nose with her index finger and added, "Not my patient. Got it?"

Watching the friends' banter, feeling the comradery, mutual respect, and love they had for one another awoke the demons of his past. Desperate to drag him back into their bottomless pit of despair, desperation, and gut-wrenching loss, the bastards' favorite place to torment him with the future they'd gladly taken from him, Sable attempted to fight, to maintain his cover...to escape.

Holding his breath, his waning power not strong enough to hold off the fiends and keep him hidden, the Paladin reluctantly relented. *Blurry images of men dressed in black leather, their masks, gloves, and chest plates adorned with all manner of silver spikes, barbs, and ragged-edged thorns attacked his broken mind.*

Days bled into months that became years which amassed into decades of endless torture, untold horrors, and a total loss of control that left him bereft and empty. Unable to stop the barrage of nightmares, he fell headlong into a vortex of dark, murky, soul-sucking recollections.

There was no rhyme nor reason, no logical order. Nothing fit together. It was a haze of agony sent from Satan himself to continue the brutality his minions had started. Blurred images, unintelligible growls, squawking barks, the staticky snap of the whip, the sizzling burn of the silver - it all culminated into the acrid stench of burning flesh... his flesh... infiltrating his senses.

Plummeting to a halt that felt like an iron fist to the gut then spinning as if he were strapped to a merry-go-round, visions of days and nights buried in the snow, unable to move, freezing to death bombarded his unstable psyche. There was no escape. There was no Hope. The soul of his Dragon King had given his final farewell. Waiting was the hardest part. Nothing worth having ever came without an outrageous price.

Resigned to his fate, actually glad the pain would finally come to an end, Sable did the only thing he could... he counted his blessings. Wasn't that what his màthair had always told them to do? Wasn't that the teachings of the Ancients? Wasn't that why he above all others was chosen?

And he'd done what he had to do. He'd kept his oath.

The Overlords had miserably failed. They were no match for his determination. The Rún Naofa was safe. Enemies of the Dragons would never know.

Stone, his twin, the other half of his very being, was safe. He was with his Mate, the powerful Arctisune. One-half of the Lauder brothers would have a future. The Sipsach said the future was fluid - a living being - that changed with every decision, every thought, every breath.

The price had been high, but so very worth it. Sable would take his place in the Heavens alongside his parents, his Clan, and the Ancients with a clear conscience and pure heart. He'd done what he'd been created to do.

The fucking Overlords were dead. Some killed by an incredibly corrupt and supremely demented Fairy, the others by a magical explosion, the very one responsible for Sable's new-found freedom.

For a fleeting second, he'd felt his twin's magic. Stone had been there, had been responsible for Sable's freedom. It didn't matter that he'd ended up buried under mountains of snow and ice. He was no longer in chains, no longer forced to harm innocents, no longer under the rule of violent fanatics who sought to destroy Dragonkin, all Shifters, the world if their rantings were any indication.

It had been her scent, the beat of her heart, the call of her soul to his that grabbed hold of him. It forced him to fight. Demanded he not give up but be the Dragon he was meant to be. Destiny, the wretched sister to Fate, dangled the smallest glimmer of hope just out of his reach. She put the Tigress in that gorge, on that day to make Sable realize what was truly at stake...a real life.

If only he deserved it. If only he could forget. If only...

Fighting the black magic coursing through his veins, he clawed through the ice and snow. Dragging his body across the jagged layers of ice, he'd gotten as close as possible to the surface, before passing out.

Covered in a thick layer of hoarfrost that cracked and immediately refroze with his every movement, his entire body went numb. His every joint and muscle ceased to function. His brain sent the demands, but his limbs refused to obey.

His Dragon King, Herne cursed, "Ah did nae return jist fur ye tae die. Wake up, Welp. Wake up an' fight."

No sooner had the gruff old Monarch's voice slashed through his mind than the massive paws of Lore's Tigress cleared away the slush. Her large jowls closed tenderly around his upper arm and with one mighty jerk, she'd pulled him out.

Too much...it was all too much. A fragmented mind, he could repair. A shattered soul, he could mend. Broken bones, torn tendons, ripped muscles, he could heal. All of it at once, heaped high with the guilt of the past and the realization that he would never know the love of his Mate, was simply too much. It was unbearable, inconceivable, and stopped his heart in his chest.

Unable to do anything but fall, Sable waited for his bone-crushing introduction to the stone floor. He held his breath, knowing how badly it would hurt.

But it never came.

Instead, his body landed on a safe, warm cocoon of soft, silky fur. Blacking out, what little was left of his consciousness falling into the darkness, his body once again betrayed him. Shaking so hard his teeth chattered, and his bones rattled, the last drop of Herne's magic evaporated just as the voice of the Leopard shot through Sable's mind, *"There! I found him. Now, get the son of a bitch off my back."*

CHAPTER THREE

"He's not breathing!"

Pulling him onto the floor, she crawled towards his head while ordering a now furless Minka, "Start chest compressions. He's not dying on my watch."

Sliding her hand under his neck and tilting his chin upward, Lore laid her hand on his forehead and leaned forward, immediately starting mouth-to-mouth resuscitation. Touching her lips to his, she pulled back with such force that she landed on her ass as she screamed, "Son of a bitch! That hurt!"

"What?!" Minka shrieked. "Is the dude radioactive?"

"No! Keep doing chest compressions."

"Yes, ma'am, Boss Lady. Whatever you say, Boss Lady. I live to serve..."

Tuning out her best friend's sass, Lore was immediately back up on her knees. Thighs against the Dragon's ribcage, she inserted the first two fingers on each hand gently into his mouth and slowly pushed. Opening his jaw just enough to see inside, she worked to figure out what had just burnt the inside of her mouth and throat.

Finally answering Minka's original question while the Leopard was still bitching in time to the beat of her hands pushing on the Dragon's chest, Lore huffed, "Not radioactive. I'm pretty sure... I just need to..." Unable to continue speaking and achieve her goal, the Tigress extended her index finger, immediately jerking it back and yelping, "Dammit! That burns!"

Up on her feet and racing to the instrument drawer on the far wall, she grabbed the jaw spreader she used for large predators, a pair of forceps, and her largest tin snips, all while Minka ramblingly demanded, "What the fuck is going on? Is he dead or alive? Why are you hopping around like a Dixie Mountain Toad running from a Coyote? Are you ever going to answer me? Should I still be trying to break this guy's ribs? Is he alive or dead?" Taking a huge gasping breath, she ended with a wailing, "COULD YOU JUST FUCKING ANSWER ME?"

Frantically nodding as she inserted the jaw spreader, Lore breathily reassured, "Keep his blood pumping to all the vital organs. He's alive... kinda sorta. I think I know..." Hearing the jingle of her forceps against whatever had stung her tongue, she growled, "What in all the holy fuckinations?"

"Holy what? What are you babbling about?" Spitting out words like bullets from a Tommy gun, Minka just kept going. "Please don't tell me you haven't gone mad? We'll all be screwed! What the crap's in there? Did he eat bad... Wait! What do Dragons eat?"

"Give. Me. A..." Lore breathed.

Maneuvering the instrument to get a better hold, she closed the pointed tips around the offending object. Holding it as steady as she could while lowering the tin snips into what little space there was in the Dragon's mouth, she slid the bottom blade between the shining band and the tender flesh of his tongue. Inhaling deeply then holding her breath, she quickly snapped the razor-sharp edges together.

The very split-second she heard the *crack* of the metal, Lore ripped it from his mouth and whipped her head to the side. Holding the offending material in the space between her face and Minka's she snarled, "They cut off his tongue and stuck a fucking band of silver around it so it couldn't grow back."

Mouth open, eyes as wide as saucers, Minka sputtered, "It's evil... It was... How the fu...? What the he...?"

"Exactly!" Lore fumed. Back up on her feet, she zipped around to the head of the bed and bent over. "Stop the compressions and grab his legs."

"Okay," Minka agreed a bit too easily, a sure sign she was beyond freaked out.

As soon as her friend had her hands securely underneath the Dragon's knees, Lore instructed, "We're taking him to the gurney." When his back hit the table, she spun towards the door and hollered over her shoulder, "Strap the restraints on his wrists and ankles and put the leather belt across his waist."

Throwing open the doors of the wall-to-wall cabinet, she dug through the boxes and containers until her hand landed on the handle of the defibrillator, she used on only her largest patients. Jerking it into the glaring fluorescent lights, she spun on her toes and dashed back to the table.

In a matter of seconds, the machine was plugged in and turned on, and the high-pitched whir of the motor revving up was bouncing all around the room. Pouring gel on both the paddles, Lore nodded to Minka, "Clear."

No sooner had the Leopard jumped backward than Lore slammed the paddles onto the Dragon's chest and pushed the buttons with her thumbs. Counting to three as his body shook and his back bowed off the table, she lifted the amplified electrodes and pressed the first two fingers of her left hand to his carotid artery.

With no evident pulse, she repeated the process again and again until on the fourth attempt; she finally felt a faint bump against her fingertips. Letting out the breath she'd been holding since she pulled the silver band welded around the Dragon's tongue from his mouth, she looked up at Minka and hissed, "We need to x-ray his chest. Something doesn't sound right."

Not waiting for an answer, she all but tossed the portable defibrillator onto the instrument tray to the side and jogged to the foot-end of the cot. Waving her hand as she pushed the gurney towards the door, she spoke before Minka could and huffed, "Ya' wanna give me a hand steering this damned thing? He weighs about three times as much as I do, and we haven't oiled these frikkin' wheels in forever."

Once again, going along with the plan without a smart-assed comment, Lore was forced to temper her tone and ask, "You okay?"

Shaking her head so quickly that her long blond ponytail whipped from side-to-side, the Leopard spat, "Hell no. In no way, shape, or form am I okay. But I'll wait to lose my shit until you have time to talk me down then explain what in the fires of Hades is going on."

"Ok..."

"And it better be one whopper of a tale. I love ya' and all, but *da-yum* woman. You have the worst taste in men."

Barking out a laugh despite the situation, Lore followed as Minka maneuvered the gurney into the iron-lined cubicle explicitly designed for the best veterinary imaging machine money could buy. Stopping under the large metal cube that housed the actual camera, the Tigress grabbed the handles and placed the lens right over the Dragon's torso.

Moving so quickly that everything around her was little

more than a blur, Lore sprinted into the tech station, flipped the switches, twisted the dials, and moved the screen so she could see the images in real time. Holding the joystick, she depressed the button on the top. Moving centimeter by centimeter, she took one picture after another trying to get every view possible in order to confirm her suspicions.

Lost in thought, letting the images on the screen meld with her hypothesis, Lore jumped at least a foot off the floor when Minka pointed and gasped, "Holy schnickeys! Is that what I think it is?"

Hating that she'd been right in her assumptions and holding back the tears for a man she'd just met but longed to know better, Lore sniffled, "Yes."

"But why would..."

Suddenly overtaken with a rage unlike anything she'd ever before felt and the need to avenge a man who'd been through more than she could ever imagine, her hand tightened on the camera control so tightly the sound of cracking plastic filled the booth. Slowly turning to face her friend, the Tigress growled through gritted teeth, "Why would someone implant two-inch silver spikes throughout his entire body? And why would they place them where they would cause the most pain but not kill him? Is that what you're asking?"

"Yeah," Minka mumbled with a nod. "That about sums it up."

Turning her eyes back to the Dragon she knew she would follow through the fires of Hell, she snarled, "Fuck it all if I know, but Goddess have mercy on their souls, 'cause when I find 'em, I'm gonna make 'em pay."

CHAPTER FOUR

*D*rifting towards consciousness, floating on a cloud of blessed peace, Sable felt the first solace he'd known in decades. The total lack of pain. It was the first time he could recall that every single cell of his body wasn't screaming in agony.

"I'm finally dying. The end is so near I can almost feel it," he mouthed words as he thought them, not daring to make a sound as the inside of his jaws felt like raw meat from the weeping scabs and his throat raw to the point of bleeding from centuries of continuous silver poisoning.

The words continued to circle his mind right up until he gasped aloud. Disconcerting to say the least, but not altogether uncomfortable, the feel of his rejuvenated tongue rubbing against his teeth was a pleasant surprise. It was merely an incredibly odd sensation to have it back after so very many years.

"Fully restored. Just as it is written in the Book of the Ancients. 'So we came into the world in the perfect image of our Creator, so shall we return to the Heavens.'."

Riding the waves of Peace, he sighed what he was sure

was his last breath. Sinking farther into the soft warmth that cradled him in safety and allowed his soul a respite from the pain, he curled farther into the sanctuary of his own making.

But he couldn't move.

Immediately drenched in cold sweat, his muscles spasmed with uncontrollable terror. The icy fingers of dread crept down his spine, his teeth dug into his newly reformed tongue, and his eyes rolled back in his head.

Then came the rage.

Scorching, fiery, deranged madness. Festering in his soul, feeding on his hourly beatings, constant degradation, and endless torment, it rose like a venomous Kraken its tentacles reaching in every direction, grabbing him around the neck and chest and dragging him into its murky depths. For as long as he could remember, Sable had allowed the pain and welcomed the torture, knowing he was doing it for the greater good, but this time, the last fucking time, the bastards had gone too far.

He wasn't free. He wasn't dying. He wasn't anything but a fucking plaything for the slithering, spineless vermin of the world.

It had *all* been a dream. A sick, twisted fantasy created by his maniacal captors to torment and brutalize him. They'd fucked with his mind time and time again but never had they tricked him into believing he could finally die. Never had they been able to dig so deeply into his subconscious that they could create a mirage of the very woman created just for him, the only woman he would ever love, his one, true Fated Mate.

They'd crossed a line he hadn't even known was there but thanked the Heavens, the Universe and the Goddess he'd finally reached. He had absolutely nothing else to lose.

Stone was safe, of that Sable was sure. It was the only thing he would swear to. He'd felt his brother's magic, knew his twin had caused the massive malignant machination of black magic to explode, and that meant their Clan was also safe. The fucking Overlords had nothing and no one left to threaten him with. They'd played their last fucking card and came up short.

Focusing every ounce of energy, every molecule of magic, and the very flames of his Dragon on the single unblemished, glowing flicker of light in the very pit of his soul, Sable thrust the gift the Universe had given him as one of her Chosen Warriors into the brilliant glow. Instantaneously feeling the essence of the Ancients, the quintessence of his Dragon King empowering every cell of his body, he struck with the intensity of a wild animal.

In one fluid motion, powered with the single-minded determination that he would *never* die lying down, the Paladin ripped his wrists and ankles from the restraints, catapulting straight into the air. Blinded by fury, wrapped in a mindless frenzy, his every action leaped from his instinctual, undeniable need for revenge. The blessed release of death could wait. The bastards had poked the Dragon, and now they would feel his wrath.

It was liberating in a way he'd never imagined. Decades upon decades he'd been forced to endure whatever they threw at him to keep his brother, his Clan, and the *Rún Naofa* safe, but no more.

No. Fucking. More.

He would go to the Heavens stained with the blood of his enemies. The fight would be brutal. There would be no coming back. He would die. They would die. Fate and Destiny be damned.

Welcoming the flames of transformation dancing down his spine, he felt his lips curl in the evilest of grins as his flesh melted and melded into the impenetrable scales of his Dragon King. Flowing over his arms, down his spine, and around his legs, Sable welcomed the renewed honor of being one with his Dragon.

Bathed in crimson, his vision narrowed. Charging across the vast open space in less than a single heartbeat, he ripped the massive metal door from its hinges. Ignoring the blaring alarms and roar of Herne demanding he take heed; the Paladin slammed his impervious mental blocks in place and sped forward.

Climbing the metal stairs three at a time, the intricate grate ripping at the battered skin on the bottom of his feet, he tore through yet another mechanical door. Throwing off all manner of smells, sounds, and screaming emotions that battered his senses, he barreled towards the sound of quarreling voices.

"Stop!" The voice of his Dragon King shook the confines of his mind. *"Stop yer shite reit this minute, ye daft welp."*

Reinforcing his mental shielding, refusing to be led astray ever again, he let the last semblance of his humanity fade away. Caught in the chaos, relishing the freedom of once and for all fighting back, he stampeded down the dark, winding hall. Acting purely on instinct, his huge taloned paw reached out of its own accord. Closing tight around the soft flesh of the neck of the first person he came to, Sable lifted the small, insignificant being off the ground and shook its tiny body.

Shoving his face so close to his adversary that the crunch of bone and the coppery scent of blood filled his senses as the end of his shortened snout crushed the other person's nose, he glared at the closed eyelids of the fiend, and he squeezed ever tighter as he growled, "Any last words?"

Barking with laughter as tears wet the coward's cheeks, Sable taunted, "Crying? Are you gonna beg, too? A fucking coward to the very end."

Then just like that, in the blink of an eye, time stood still. The eyes of the person dangling from his clenched fist popped open. Caught in the anguished stare of one blue and one brown eye, Sable's heart ceased to beat.

How could it be? How could he have been so wrong? What was real? What had he done? Could it be?

Reaching out with his free hand as he loosened the steel grip he had on her neck, his only thought was to pull her close and beg for forgiveness, but that was not meant to be. Leaning forward, needing to catch her falling body before it hit the floor, Sable instead found himself roaring as the all-too-familiar sensation of silver thrusting into his flesh set his back on fire.

Unable to stop his forward movement, everything suddenly moving in slow motion, he slammed into the ground at the exact same moment as his Mate. Opening his mouth to apologize, nothing came out; only bubbling spatters of blood and a sickeningly wet wheeze where his voice should have been.

Trying once again, it was his turn to shed tears as she struggled to her knees, laid her hand on his cheek and painfully croaked, "Breathe, damn you, breathe. Don't you dare fucking die on me again."

CHAPTER FIVE

*F*alling into the chair against the wall, she pulled off her rubber gloves, wadded them up in a ball, and shot them into the hazardous waste bin in the far corner of her newly equipped recovery room. Glancing at the clock, she exhaled sharply before counting aloud, "Two, three, four long fucking hours." Letting her eyes fall back to her patient, she added, "That's three you owe me now, Dragon. Three times I've brought you back from Death's door."

What was it about him? Why had she been invested in his survival since the first sniff of smoky cherry wood blowing on a blustery breeze in the middle of the frozen tundra? Something in the back of her mind was screaming for her to wake the hell up and pay attention, cursing at her for being an idiot, but Lore was too tired, too pissed, and too worried to pay attention. If things would ever slow down for longer than two seconds, maybe she'd have time to think about precisely what was happening.

"And that will happen when snowmen decorate the Gates of Hell."

The squeak of rubber boot soles scuffing the tile floor in

the main part of the clinic announced Minka's approach. Watching the door, she worked on her smile, and the Leopard murmured, "How's he doin'?"

"Pretty good. Really good actually." Take a shaking breath; she added with more authority and confidence, "He'll be fine. He's strong. Hell, he's a fucking Dragon. If he can't take a stab or a hundred with silver..." Knowing her attempt at easing her friend's tension was falling apart with every syllable she uttered, Lore bit her tongue and shut up.

Rolling her head one way and then the other, working to dispel the massive knots of tension and fatigue eating away at her neck and shoulders, she took a deep breath and tried again, "He's gonna be fine. How are *you* doin'?"

"I'm okay," Minka shrugged, crossing the threshold and slowly making her way to the chair beside Lore. "I just can't believe..."

"You were doin' what comes naturally," Jewel, veterinarian nurse extraordinaire and seriously powerful magical being, interrupted, her melodious voice filling the room as she entered and scurried to check the Dragon's vitals. "We can't fight instinct. You saw your best friend in danger, and did what Leopards do, jumped in to save her."

As usual, Jewel, the only Nymph who dared to live anywhere near the asscrack of the universe, who also just happened to be the best fucking health care professional - as she liked to be called - Lore had ever worked with, used *her* unique brand of magic to diffuse the regret and sadness swirling around the room. Sitting on the Tigress' other side, she touched Lore's shoulder, signaling that she was going to lean in for a closer look.

Lightly touching the healing skin of Lore's neck, Jewel happily reported, "And you're healin' nicely, too." Turning forward in her chair, she slapped the tops of her legs, cheerfully announcing, "A good night's work was had by all. Minka saved the Doc, and the Doc saved the Dragon."

"Something she wouldn't have had to do if I'd taken just a bloody second to let my wee brain engage."

Smiling at the way Minka's proper British accent got stronger the longer she spoke, Lore did her best, albeit horrible because she still carried her Texas drawl from years studying at UT, impression of Eliza Doolittle with the hopes of lifting her best friend's mood. "Aww, you're just a wanker without a clue. We're all good."

Shaking her head, the smallest of smiles curling the sides of her mouth, Minka's eyes met Lore's for the first time since she'd entered the room. "That was the absolute worst."

"I know," Lore admitted before laughing out loud. "Ya' know I suck at accents of any kind, and I'll leave the impressions to Dana Carvey."

"Your southern twang overrides damn near *everything*." Chuckling, Jewel added with her original Scottish brogue, "Yoo're a bonnie lass an' aw, jist stick tae th' doctorin' an' yoo'll be alreit."

The longer she laughed, the better Lore felt. Her favorite professor in medical school always said laughter was the best medicine, and dammit all, that old geezer had never been wrong.

"Okay, okay, I give." Raising her hands in mock surrender, she laid on her Texas drawl just as thick as she could. "Y'all know I suck at anything but bein' me. So, it's a damned good thing y'all like me as I am."

"Oh, my Goddess, if you say fiddle-dee-dee or I do declare, I swear I might toss my cookies right here," Minka chortled. "When you go deep south, I imagine that scene at the end of Gone with the Wind. I wait for you to put your hand on your forehead and say, "With God as my witness, I'll never go hungry again."

"'Frankly, my dear, I don't give a damn' is more her speed," Jewel chirped, so tickled with her own joke that her usually lavender curls turned a bright pink and the pointed tips of her ears wiggled with glee as her giggle turned into full-blown laughter.

"Well, I'm damned glad I'm here for y'all's amusement."

"And so are we," the ladies cackled in unison.

Sitting and laughing with her friends was just what the doctor ordered ~ for all of them. So much so, that when it was time to check the Dragon's vital signs, Lore felt well enough to do it herself.

Getting to her feet, she made a shooing motion with her hand, and in the closest thing she had to a commanding tone, ordered, "Y'all get upstairs and get some sleep. I can handle things here for the next four or five hours." Nodding towards the Dragon, she went on, "I don't feel comfortable leaving him alone until he's at least opened his eyes for the first time." Quickly forcing away the memories of the first time she'd seen his eyes, she went on, "Or the second time, or whatever...Oh dammit, y'all know what I mean."

"You're the one who needs..."

Cutting off Jewel's objection, she leveled her gaze and slowly shook her head. "Yeah, and so do you." Pointing towards the door, she added, "Now, get outta here. I'll come to get you when it's your turn."

Turning back towards the Dragon and pointedly ignoring her friends' grumbles, Lore waited until Minka and Jewel were out of the recovery room and heard the sound of the first mechanical door opening and closing before uncovering her patient. Finding the two six-inch incisions on his lower back healing quickly, even more so than she'd expected, she removed the sutures and put the blanket back over him.

Changing out the bag of IV fluids she prayed would help flush the silver from his body, she couldn't stop thinking about the overabundance of Celtic runes covering his skin. While she'd been removing the tips of Minka's silver spikes from his kidneys, Lore neutralized the living, breathing black magic feeding each glyph, making it impossible for them to continue their devilish mission. She'd also neutralized the copious amounts of high-grade silver infused in ink. However, the trouble someone had gone to inflict an eternity of pain on this one Dragon continued to eat away at her soul.

Not only were the runes *ancient*, old as time, scary as hell, but the magic in them was not only black as night, it was downright immoral, an abomination of plague proportions that had been 'birthed'...*implanted*. Living, breathing, evolving, growing, it had been created especially and specifically for Sable with the express purpose of learning everything about the Dragon and eventually *become* him. How he'd been able to not only survive but keep the obscene devilry at bay was nothing short of wondrous.

She could feel the Dragon of his soul. The poor old guy was subdued, harnessed by heinous witchcraft every bit as powerful and evil as the runes covering the Paladin. It was unimaginable the torture a King as powerful as he had suffered, not being able to protect the man with whom he shared his soul.

Whoever had done this had help...huge, massive, god or demon-like assistance. That person had sold their soul and millions of others to tap into enough shit sorcery to hold not only a Guardsman but a centuries-old Dragon. She could only pray that if she helped the man, he could help the King with whom he shared his very being.

"At least I was able to reinforce the white magic ones. I'm prayin' that keeps you safe," she mumbled to herself, letting the tips of her fingers gloss over the magnificent image of a Dragon spanning from one shoulder blade to the other.

Sparks of electricity combined with a recognition that

called to not only the heart and soul of the woman but also that of the huge Siberian Tigress with whom she shared her very being, zipped and zinged through her body. Memories, not her own but those of the Dragon's, began to form. Pictures of people she'd never before seen but somehow knew, places she'd never been but somehow recalled, the distinct scents and sounds of it all melded together then flickered and flashed until ultimately coalescing into a movie running on fast forward through her mind.

Blurring past so quickly she couldn't see anything but stripes of color, she tried again and again to pull her hand from his back, to somehow break the connection she believed was causing their telepathic bond, but nothing worked. Heart pounding faster and faster, her breathing changed to panting as sweat poured down her back.

Something was coming. Something big, bad, and ugly. Something evil and full of hate. Something bringing death and destruction. Something with its sights set on the Dragon...and now on her.

Summoning the magic she'd inherited from her maternal grandmother, Lorelai Ashevak - the Shaman of her people, blessed by the Great Mother, and given the power of the Spirits - she flooded the bond with ancient Inuit mysticism. Calling forth her Tigress, watching as thick, white fur adorned with ebony stripes covered the back of her hand and rose up her arm, a warmth she'd never before experienced filled the palm of her hand.

Reassuring, fortifying, the heat worked its way up the underside of her arm and across her chest, surrounding her heart with a feeling of completion. Downright unnerved, quickly approaching freaked out, she whispered what little she could remember of the prayer her grandmother had taught her. "O' Great Mother, whose voice I hear on the winds, and whose breath gives life to all the world, please hear my words, please hear my plea. I am small, and I am weak. Your loving strength and your loving wisdom are all I ask to make the darkness flee."

Instantly able to lift her hand, she'd barely gotten to breathe when her eyes went wide, and her heart skipped a beat. Turning her arm all the way over, she could only gawk at the thin layer of sparkling granite Dragon scales covering her skin.

Blowing out the breath she hadn't realized she'd been holding, Lore forced herself to look down at the Dragon. Eyes scanning the patrician slope of his nose, the perfect bow of his lips, and the masculine line of his jaw, her eyes landed on the tattoo flowing along his collarbone in bold, beautiful script.

"Beul-aithris" She said the word aloud. "I should know that word. I've heard it some...Jewel!" She yelped. "It's Scottish. It's... It means... Oh dammit, I know this. It means..."

"It means Lore." The Dragon's deep, resonate baritone rolled over and through her like hundred-year-old Scotch.

Eyes flying to his, she was shocked to see them closed, and even more surprised at the lax muscles of his face and the slow, rhythm of his breathing. Leaning closer, her cheek hovering just above the sheet, her lips scant inches from his, she whispered, "I hope you're talking in your sleep, Dragon. If not, it's official, I've gone straight down the fucking rabbit hole, and I'm takin' you with me."

CHAPTER SIX

"*Come on, Lorelei. Time to go before your mother comes looking for us.*"

"*Dad!*" *The little dark-haired girl complained, her long black ponytails swinging back and forth as they hung out from under her woolen cap. "Lorelei is grandma's name. I'm Lore. L-O-R-E. Lore.*"

Although barely three-foot tall and sporting the chubby cheeks of youth, the child exuded the inner strength and confidence of a leader. Running towards her father, she transformed into an adorable while also being formidable miniature white Tigress, the shadow of her newly forming stripes traversing her back.

Launching herself at the man's back, the Cub's ferocious growl turned into playful chuffs and giddy trills as her father spun on his heels, caught her in midair, and pulled her belly to his chest. Letting his hands transform into those of his own Tiger, he tousled the fur on her back and across her head. Swatting his beard-covered jaw and chin with paws, careful not to unsheathe her claws, the Cub made all manner of yips and chirps, her enthusiasm for their play-fighting growing by the second.

Dropping to his knees and completing his transformation, her father rolled onto his back, making a show of letting his daughter get the best of him. Panting, the beat of her racing heart filling the frosty air, the little girl threw back her head, her high-pitched roar announcing to all that she was the victor.

Sable had never seen anything as beautiful, as wonderful, as life-affirming as watching the father and his daughter enjoying life not only as humans but as Tigers. Wanting to tell them how much they inspired him, the Guardsman lifted his foot to step forward as he opened his mouth to announce his intention.

"Hello," he called to the Tigers, surprised when they gave no indication of hearing his greeting or smelling his scent.

Stepping closer, wanting to let them know he was friend and not foe, Sable raised his voice, once again announcing, "Hi there. Name's Sable and I wanted..."

Stopping mid-stride, his heart dropping like a stone into water, the Guardsman stood still. Looking at his ungloved hands and bare chest and feet, reality reared his ugly head.

"I'm not actually here," he murmured under his breath. "It sure as hell feels real." Bending down, he touched the snow. "Feels real." Rubbing his thumb and forefinger together, he scoffed, "Damn sure wet and cold." Slowly standing up, he shook his head. "Dream sharing. Strongest I've ever experienced, even with Stone."

With the words still echoing through his mind, his disappointment turned to elation. The bond he shared with his Mate was growing, strengthening, pulling them closer together. It was miraculous in its symbolism and poignant in its validity. Something he prayed she was feeling as powerfully as he was. It would help her understand why he had to leave, why he had to...

WHUMPH! An uproar something like a twenty-pound sack of potatoes falling from a fifty-foot height straight into a three-foot vat of baby powder swallowed the rest of his thought. Eyes trained on the Tigers as they jumped to their paws and sprinted away from the sound, Sable saw nothing but a white streak flying over the snow.

Flying alongside father and daughter, so invested in their safety, the Guardsman was caught entirely unaware when the male Tiger telepathically roared, "Avalanche!" Scanning the landscape, looking for safe passage for his daughter, he continued, "Run towards the Forest, Sweet Kulu. Take cover in the skeletons of the trees."

"NO! No, Atâta," she snarled. "I stay with you."

Growling low in his throat, the huge Tiger roared, "Lorelei!" Breath visible in the frigid air as he sharply exhaled before continuing with unconditional love and adoration coloring his tone. "Please, Akuluk. Please do as I say. I will come for you, my sweet one. I promise."

Gazing at her father for a split-second longer before breaking off as instructed, Sable watched in wonder as the Cub tore across the Tundra. Heart nearly beating out of her chest, fear for her mother and her grandmother who were so very close to the origin of the spine-tingling howl of Mother Nature forced tears to wet the light gray fur of her muzzle.

The faster she ran and the farther from the avalanche she got, the more her fear combined with a nightmarish terror. Shaking with the need to protect her, the talons of his Dragon King breaking through the tips of his fingers and digging into the palm of his hand, Sable fought the limitations of the dream world, cursing within his own mind at his blasted restraints.

Then her voice, the timbre of which should have been small and tinny, broke through the haze of his own thoughts. Robust, resilient, irrepressible - her strength once again astounded him, even as her words revealed what she dreaded most.

"I will not fear the Shadows. I will not fear the Dead. I will not fear the Shadows. I will not fear the Dead. The Goddess is with me. I am a child of the Great Mother. My heart beats with the blood of Nunam. I enter the Forest of my own free will. My ancestors resting there will welcome and protect me."

Paws pounding closer and closer to a dark, dense mass of petrified trees, decayed wreckage, and a shroud of death that burrowed into his subconscious and ate at his soul, the Tigress never faltered.

Cutting through the mist and fog, she crossed the border without hesitation.

Weaving around the broken remains of tree trunks, maneuvering past the unearthed remains of ships lost at sea when the world was still young, she gave a wide berth to a surprisingly immaculate structure. From one heartbeat to the next, Sable's memories super-imposed over the child's. No longer was he only looking through her eyes, but also his own from a jarringly recent past.

"I've been here. Bled here. Died here." Glancing to the right, he recognized the dilapidated shack where his twin had been tortured. Turning in a complete circle, he saw the tents left by the Overlords during their hasty retreat. The very place where they'd cut out his tongue and flayed the flesh from his bones. How could...?

Jerked back into the Tigress' recollections, seeing everything from her perspective once again as a deep growling rumble rose from the very center of the earth. Growing exponentially with every millisecond ticked by, it expanded in depth and width, came from every direction, and shook the ground from both above and below.

Skidding to a stop, her claws deep in the ice, the Cub's tail took the lead, whipping her body in a half-circle. Stopped cold, her wide-eyed stare stuck on the great plumes of glistening white snow exploding upward towards the Heavens, she instantly dropped to her belly. Throwing back her brilliant white head, she lifted her muzzle to the sky, emitting a heart-wrenching howl that had tears streaming down the Dragon's face.

What seemed like hours, but only took a few moments had been life-altering not only for the little Tigress but for Sable. Changed on an elemental, soul-deep level, he watched as she effortlessly transformed back into the little girl, got to her feet, and slowly walked into the mausoleum.

Whooshing through the ether, flung across the threshold, he watched from the shadows as she walked straight to the altar and knelt before the wooden Cross. Laying her hands on the stone surface, careful not to touch but to get as close as she possibly could to the intricately carved figurines of the animals, he held his breath as her head fell forward.

Moments passed, time during which Sable still dared not to breathe. Then he heard it, her clear resonant voice, heavy with sorrow but laced with steely determination. "Today the world has changed along with my part in it. Today I pray for those I love and hope to see them again. But if that is not my Destiny, if Fate has other plans, I thank you, Great Mother, that I have lived to see your wonders and the light that fills the world."

CHAPTER SEVEN

*I*nhaling the wonderfully warm scent that was all man with just the right dash of Dragon, she sunk into the exhilarating tingle spreading throughout her body. It didn't matter that her butt was asleep or that the muscles in her back ached from sleeping in such an odd position, Lore had no doubt she was pretty damned close to Heaven.

So tired she couldn't keep her eyes open, she used the excuse of needing to be near her patient to pull a chair to the side of his bed. As if that hadn't been telling enough, she'd slid her fingers between his and laid her head on the bed next to his arm telling the walls that she was, *"Only doing it to keep track of his vitals."*

"And if you believe that, I've got some swamp land I'll sell ya' for cheap," she snickered to her still-resting patient.

Keeping her eyes closed, rejecting the idea of ending the best night of sleep she'd had in longer than she cared to remember, the Tigress listened to the steady beat of the Dragon's heart. Drifting on a cloud of peaceful relaxation, images of her dream slowly resurfaced.

Suddenly unsettled, she let the fantasy play out. Gripping

the Dragon's hand tighter the more vivid the images became, she swiped at the tears wetting her cheeks.

"This isn't... That's not..." Unable to complete a thought. Troubled by what she saw, but knowing she had to reach a conclusion if she was ever to figure out what her mind was trying to show her, Lore popped up straight and with her eyes wide open.

Gaze going straight to the Dragon's face, for the first time, she stopped fighting her instincts and let her mind join with his. She had no way of knowing how, but she just knew that the answers to the changes in her dreams lay within the chaos she'd felt churning within him.

Still holding tight to his hand, she slowly let the shielding in her mind fall open. Little by little, she took in the true scope of this one man's supremacy.

Barely able to keep her bearings as a barrage of angry, horrible, downright gruesome images assaulted her mind, Lore refused to look away. If he had physically and mentally endured such barbarity in his real life, the least she could do was witness them as mere mental pictures. Stopping the fast-forward recreation when it became so heart-wrenching, so depraved, that she had to see it as it actually happened, she inhaled deeply and let it begin again – this time at normal speed.

Ears ringing at the crack of the cat-of-nine-tails on the already shredded skin of his back, the claws of her Tigress erupted through the tips of her fingers as she felt the silver barbs ripping through the muscle. Growls bubbling up from her chest, she stood helpless, an insubstantial voyeur to the pain these heathens had inflicted upon a man who refused to relent.

Digging the silver spikes sewn into the fingertips of his black leather gloves into the flesh of the Dragon's jaws, the Overlord spat in his face before snarling, "Tell me the truth. Speak the ancient words and end your suffering."

Glaring at his captor, the golden flecks in his deep hazel eyes glowing with an unspent vengeance, the Paladin stayed silent. More enraged, his abysmal failure evident, the savage thug lost all control.

"All of you," he roared to his cohorts. "Thrash him! Beat him! Whip him! Rip the flesh from his bones! MAKE THIS FUCKING DRAGON BLEED!"

Seven men at his back and two at his front, the Overlords beat, punched, whipped, and tortured the Paladin until he no longer resembled a man, but the dead carcass of an animal after being pecked at by the Ravens. Covered in blood and gore, the barbarians filed out of the room laughing at what they'd done, the leader calling over his shoulder, "We'll be back as soon as you've healed, Dragon."

Arms stretched over his head, the silver of his shackles eating away at what little flesh still covered his wrists, the Paladin continued to stare forward. Not moving a muscle, every ounce of his nearly seven-foot, muscular frame balanced on the very tip of his toes, the magic - an ancient, pure, white mysticism, as old as time, and as strong as the Universe Herself swirled into view.

Swirling like a cyclone, turning red then yellow before switching to purple and finally settling on a calm, frosty tone of blue, the mist found its shape. All motion stopped, time quite literally stood still, and there before the Dragon appeared Flidais, the Lady of the Forest.

Walking forward, her elegant hand reaching towards him, the Goddess of the Hunt brushed his battered skin with the very tips of her fingers. With tears cascading down her cheeks, she whispered, "My poor child, what have they done to you?"

Unable to answer, his face and lips so swollen Lore wondered how he was even breathing, the Dragon blinked the one eye he could still hold open in response. Letting her hand fall to his shoulder, the Earth Mother nodded, "You are a brave and valiant Warrior, Sable Lauder. Your sacrifice will not go without honor and blessing."

Walking around his body, she continued, "No other has ever protected Our secret with such diligence and sacrifice. Do not fear that you have been forgotten. The end is nigh. The courier of your escape has been dispatched. You only need to wait for your own reflection."

Suddenly agitated, fighting his bonds, and thrashing his head from side-to-side, the Dragon begged through swollen lips, "No, sweet Earth Mother, please, please, anything but that."

Laying her finger to his lips, she murmured, "It is the Universe's fondest wish. Not even I can stop what has already begun."

Again, he fought. Struggling to open his mouth farther, to project from his ravaged throat, the Dragon's contention was instantly paused with a wave of the Goddess' hand. Caressing his cheek, she smiled, "Sleep, dear boy. Let the magic of my heart soothe your body as it soothes your soul. Know that I am never far."

Blinking out of sight while her words still echoed, the brilliant, glorious light of the Goddess still shone brightly. Taking her eyes off the Dragon for the first time, Lore saw the stone walls, the intricate masonry of the sarcophagi doors, the beautiful constructed alter, and the delicately carved depictions of Arctic wildlife.

"The mausoleum," she gasped, pulling out of the Dragon's mind and looking down at his striking features. "Is that why you stopped my dream? You needed me to see that we'd been in the same place?"

Placing her free hand on his chest, she leaned forward, her lips automatically going to his forehead. Gently laying kisses on his healing flesh, she whispered, "Sable. Sable Lauder." Flowing through her, filling every fiber of her being with a real sense of belonging and her heart with a joy unlike anything she'd ever felt, the sound of his name was music to her ears. Smiling against his skin, Lore breathed, "Good name."

Raising her head just enough to see his eyelids flutter, Lore held her breath, praying he was about to wake. Opening her mouth to coax him from his slumber, she instead found herself jumping backward, her protective instincts springing to life as the large double doors at the back of the room burst open.

A flash of light, an icy blast of air, and a bold wave of magic filled the room. Racing to take her stand between the Dragon and whoever dared to invade her Clinic, Lore shouted, "Stop the fucking theatrics! Show yourself!"

Out of the commotion walked an exact copy of the Dragon she was protecting with one glaring difference - the intruder's eyes were icy blue and filled with rage. Pointing the tip of his sword at Lore's heart, he demanded in a low, menacing tone, "Step back, Bitch. The games end here."

"Fuck off, Asshole!" She leaped forward, her hands instantly those of her Tigress', claws fully extended, venom dripping from their tips. "There's no way to get to him, but through me. And that's just not happening."

"We'll see about that!" Slashing his blade through the air between them as he stepped forward, the man started to speak then stopped as if he was suddenly frozen in place. Waiting for the other shoe - or sword - to fall, Lore felt her mouth drop open, and her eyes open absolutely as wide as they could as the Dragon who'd just been blissfully uncon-scious sailed right over her head before landing in front of the intruder and grabbing him by the neck.

"Back off, you Overlord scum!" The Dragon roared. "Lay a finger on my Mate, and you're a dead man."

CHAPTER EIGHT

*T*he feel of her hands on his shoulders momentarily cleared away the confusion and rage clouding what little of his good judgment remained but couldn't negate the fact that they were under attack and it was his job to protect his Mate. Caught in a bloody battle between the black abyss of his psychosis and the cold, harsh reality closing in all around him, Sable's grip tightened around the neck of the intruder.

Shaking the bastard's body, glaring into his pleading eyes, Sable roared, "Stop your fucking games! You lost! I'm free! Die, Bastard, Die!"

"Sable! Stop!" His Mate's desperate cry rocked his mind. Her pain, her fear, her utter panic clenched at his heart and stole the breath from his lungs, but still, he couldn't stop. They had said he would never get away, promised they would hunt him to the ends of the earth, but he'd been ready.

"No," he pushed through gritted teeth. "He...must...pay."

"Sable, look at me." Her words were a wave of calm across the turbulent waves of his miasmic distress. "Sable, it's me, Lore."

Her plea forced his head to turn. Ensnared by the depth of emotion in her obsidian eyes, he whispered, "Lore?"

"Yes. Lore." Her smile, a complex mix of sadness and relief, called to both man and Dragon King. It was hypnotic in its power, stirring in its depth. "Let go, Sable. You're killing..."

"*Reothadh!*"

Shooting through the vast, austere room, the power contained in that single word shook the stone foundation just under his feet. Dropping the intruder as if his skin had been scalded, Sable's head snapped forward as his arm swung behind. Holding Lore tight to his body, he snatched his sword from the ether turning them both towards the invasion, sure to shield his Mate from all harm.

Standing firm as shards from the large panes of glass shot in every direction, the Guardsman summoned the full potential of his Dragon King as hammering footsteps announced the approach of yet another foe. Sensing supremacy as ancient as his own, he wrapped Lore in a blanket of protective mysticism before taking a bold step forward.

Appearing out of chaos, dark eyes swirling with a dark silvery grey, the Nymph's glare landed on the unconscious trespasser as she repeated the Gaelic word for 'freeze' before a potent bolt of magic shot from her fingertips while she snarled, "An' stay 'at way, Boy. Ye shoold've knoon better."

Watching the heavy ebony streaks painting her long lavender hair swirling around her head like furious thunder clouds, Sable took the offensive when her fiery gaze turned on him, growling, "Not one step closer, Nymph, or I'll drop you where you stand."

Snorting with derisive laughter and rolling her eyes, she scoffed with the strong brogue of his homeland, "Ye can try if ye like, but yoo'll only be wastin' yer time." Shaking her head, the four-foot powder keg of unimaginable power took a casual step forward. "Stand doon, Sable Lauder of the Paladin Guard. Dinnae waste mah time. Mah fight isnae wi' ye. Ah only need tae make sure mah wee bonnie lassie is unharmed."

"Lore is not your concern." He snapped right at the exact moment that his Mate assured, "I'm fine, Jewel. Got it all handled."

"Not frae whaur Ah'm standin', Lass."

"Not the time," his Mate grumbled. "Just go. I've got this." Her frustration added to his own. Lore was strong, stronger than any Big Cat he'd ever known, but there was a gentleness, a true sense of caring about his welfare that softened his resolve as it added to his disorientation.

It was all too much. He had to keep Lore safe. Couldn't let the Overlords get their grimy hands on the only good thing he had left. How had they found him? How were they...

"Sable, *a bhobain,* lit me see Lore. Lit me see she's alreit 'en Ah'll go."

"What did you say?" He demanded, thrown yet another curveball by the Nymph's use of the nickname only his mother had called him.

"Ah asked ye tae lit me see my...".

"No!" He spat, his arm once again flying backward. Cutting through the protective shield he'd built around Lore; he yanked her close. "No!" Furiously shaking his head, the tip of his blade pointed at her heart, he seethed, "Not that, you lying bitch. What did you call me? Who are you? How do you know me?"

Narrowing her eyes, her ire palpable but her lips curving in a knowing smile, the Nymph nodded as she replied, "Mah name is Jewel af th' Northern Isle, jist as yoors is Sable Lauder." Taking a commanding step forward, her enchantment popping and crackling in the air around her, she continued, "Ah was thaur when ye waur born. Stone, tay." Her eyes slid to the unconscious man on the floor before snapping right back to his. "An' yer daddy, an' his daddy, an' his daddy afair heem. Noo, cut yer shite, an' let's poot thes reit." Slapping her hand across her chest, she beseeched with a low crooning voice, "It's auld Jewel. Ye knoo Ah woods ne'er hurt ye."

"Jewel?" He echoed the Nymph's response at the exact same time that his Mate yelped, "What the fuckity-fuck-fuck?"

Frantically searching his memories for any recollection of the woman standing before, Lore's bewilderment and agitation beating at his damaged psyche, pushing him to act, Sable gripped the handle of his broadsword until droplets of blood ran down his arm. Did he know her? Could she really have known his family? His Clan? His twin? Or was this another well-constructed ruse to steal the *Rún Naofa*? To rob him of what little sanity he had left?

Eyes flying to the man still motionless on the floor, he couldn't make sense of what he saw, what he felt, the aggression he'd witnessed towards his Mate. Something was wrong... very *very* wrong. Not even his Dragon King was talking.

"Herne? Herne, do I know her? Is that Stone? What is happening? Is. She. Jewel?" Words tumbling over words, one thought folding over another, he was talking so fast, so hysterically, it wasn't until the Nymph answered that he realized he was speaking aloud.

"Och, aye, tis me," the Nymph confirmed, her tone light and lyrical, no longer harsh and demanding. Reaching out to him, she smiled sweetly as radiant sparks of magic danced along her extended fingers.

Unable to decipher truth from lie, fighting against the myriad of fragmented memories pouring from the Pandora's box he'd opened in his mind, Sable held tighter still to Lore as he challenged, "Prove it."

With a single nod, the Nymph dropped her hand. Carefully watching, ready for any sleight of hand, he witnessed the last of the violence that had been churning in her eyes be instantly replaced by a soft, warm glow of understanding and adoration. The ebony stripes in her hair faded back to brilliant lavender just as the harsh white burn of her skin returned to a charming luminescence.

"See, *a bhobain*. It's just…"

"STONE!"

Slashing through the room, a venomous female battle cry swallowed up whatever the Nymph was about to say. Backing up until he knew Lore was sandwiched between his body and the concrete wall, Sable conjured another blade from the cosmos and took his stance.

Ready for all comers, his eyes flew upward as a mass of bright, white, glistening fur dropped from overhead. Moving closer, sure to move from side-to-side, he shoved his awe and wonderment aside as the mythical Arctisune landed in the empty space between where he stood and the intruder's body.

From one heartbeat to the next, she shed the body of her magical Arctic Fox, stood tall in her human form, and whipped all nine of her flaming tails to the front. Rage burned in her violet eyes as she roared, "Everybody stand the fuck down!"

"Annika?"

He heard Lore speak, but her words failed to register. This is where he would take his stand. No longer forced to endure the chains and whips of torture, he'd found his Mate. If today was his day to die, then so be it. The Secret would be safe with his Tigress.

Swinging one blade and then the other, letting the serenity of the repetitive motion calm his jagged nerves, Sable advanced. Eye-to-eye with the enemy, he refused to be retaken.

Mirroring the Vixen's moves. Sliding to the left when she went right, to the right when she went left, his only duty was to keep Lore safe. The Fox Shifter of mythical origins might be his twin's Mate, but at that moment she was his enemy.

Waiting for the perfect second to strike a blow that would incapacitate, not kill the legendary Arctisune, everything suddenly moved in slow motion. Momentarily stunned by the sight of all nine of her tails fanning out, touching the walls, ceiling, and floors - essentially cutting the room in half, Sable saw her play. Knew she was trying to back him into a corner with no chance of escape.

Tossing one of his swords back into the ether from whence it came, he grabbed Lore's hand while uttering the word, "*le chèile*."

Embracing the influx of his Mate's magic and the combination of Dragon and Tigress, he pictured the only place in the universe he ever remembered feeling safe. Spinning towards Lore, he dropped her hand, wrapped his arms around her waist, and whispered, "Hold on, *mo chroí*. I'll never let them take you."

CHAPTER NINE

*L*anding with a thud that rattled her bones, Lore dug her nails into Sable's bare shoulders and prayed the world would stop spinning. Opening her eyes, she was met with wide-eyed panic and a death grip on her hips.

"Next time give a girl a heads up before whizzing her ass through time and space," she grumbled, not at all surprised with the lack of response.

Lifting her fingers as she pressed the heels of her hands against his clavicle, Lore stepped back, at least as far as his arms would allow, before grimacing, "Ya' gotta give me a little space, 'kay? I'm not runnin' away. Just need to breathe."

When he didn't move, she raised a hand, held up her index finger and thumb about an inch apart and raising her eyebrows as far as they would go, cajoled in a tone that sounded like she was talking a kitten out of a tree, "Just for a sec, promise. Gotta get my head back on straight."

Relenting even as he looked like she'd kicked his puppy and pissed in his Cheerios, Sable's eyes turned the dreariest shade of mossy green. For a split-second, she thought about walking back into his embrace. Images of kissing away his sadness and making him forget all about the past flashed through her mind.

Shivering with excitement, her body was more than willing and all too ready, along with her big, furry alter ego, but Lore *seriously* needed a minute. Getting her shit together and formulating a plan for getting back to her Clinic topped her to-do list. The big, bad, broken Dragon Man would just have to deal.

"Yeah, you too, Tig," she grumped back at her Tigress' growl.

"I really am a bitch," she mumbled under her breath. "Minka keeps saying I've turned into an anti-social curmud- geon. Maybe she's right. Maybe I do need to get out more. Talk to people instead of animals..."

Personal introspection sucked and made her head pound like a drum line in the Homecoming parade. It was all crap she could think about later. Stuff that didn't come with easy answers.

Following her instincts, she gave Sable a quick smile before slowly turning away. "Because being whisked away by a deranged Dragon to some cave on the other side of the world can be fixed just like that," she sarcastically sighed, snapping her fingers for added effect.

Immediately entranced by the 'cave time had forgotten,' she gazed at the chalk sketches lining the stone walls. Drawn with the utmost care, each picture depicted two little boys, or *two little Dragons,* playing games, battling like Knights defending the Realm, or soaring the skies with magnificent bolts of fire flying from their mouths.

Moving farther into the darkness, the bright white of her Tigress' night vision took over allowing Lore to see the progression of the images. Spellbound by the simplistic yet beautiful depiction of the brothers as they had been when they were together, it took every ounce of her incredible strength not to turn tail and run back to Sable.

But she had to go on. Had to see where the story was leading. Had to know what had happened, who had broken the incredible bond shared by these spectacular twins.

Shuffling her feet along the ground, not wanting to disturb the toys that lay where they'd been left, the little boys' shoes neatly placed under the benches built of wood and stone, or the well-worn, wooden swords standing at attention in the corner, her hand reached out of its volition. Sparks of recognition, glimmers of enchantment skittered up her arm. It was as if the pictures were trying to speak, working to fill in the gaps, to show her the true story of Sable and Stone.

Approaching a bend in the wall of the cave, she was drawn deeper into the mystic of not only the place but of the man who had so quickly woven himself into the fabric of her being. Following the echo of a waterfall, Lore found herself walking into a grotto so spectacular, so peaceful, so breathtaking that it looked as if it's been created by the Goddess herself.

Eyes scanning the beauty, her gaze landed on another set of crudely, yet efficiently constructed benches. Smiling as she walked alongside the shimmering pool of water, it was easy to imagine the two brothers racing from one end to the other, dunking one another under the glistening waterfall, and spending hours testing out the true wonders of all their Water Dragons could do.

In the blink of an eye, real memories, the recollections of what actually happened right there in that beautiful lagoon superimposed over the reality of the moment. She could see and hear the twins laughing, playing, conspiring, murmuring, experiencing what *only* two bodies - two *souls* who'd come from one single joining could possibly share.

"He really is my Mate," she whispered to the waters. "Really is the one person made just for me."

Letting the realization she'd finally been forced to accept sink in, she walked towards the benches. Ready to take a seat and relax before heading back to Sable, she spied a tiny alcove that hadn't been visible before.

Sticking her head into the six-foot-by-six-foot stone cubby, she took in the elaborate pictures. Obviously done when the boys were older, the immaculate illustrations of their transformations into no less than five different Dragons were mind-blowing.

It was all right there. The joy they felt soaring the skies. The wonder they'd experienced exploring the depths of the sea. The majesty of being one with the Earth itself. The power of wearing armor made of scales and brandishing broadswords that were extensions of their very own bodies. The exhilaration of not only wielding but quite literally being the flames of the fire that was born in their souls. There was no doubt these boys, these Warriors had been made by the Universe for a higher purpose, and they were more than ready, willing, and able to serve in whatever way She needed.

Then came the one single illustration that caused her eyes to fill with tears and her soul to ache.

Nothing as spectacular as any of the others, this picture was nothing more than two columns of hash marks rising from the floor of the back wall of the alcove. One heading read Stone, the other Sable. Each delineation was marked with a date.

Running her fingers over the ones under her Dragon's name, Lore whispered, "Just like mom did for me, they kept track of how tall they were."

Stopping at the last line under Sable's name, the tears she'd been holding back started to fall. With her free hand, she counted eight additional markings under Stone's name.

Letting her eyes slide shut at the same time that she felt Sable at her back, Lore sobbed under her breath when he gently laid his hand over hers and murmured in awe, "He never forgot."

CHAPTER TEN

*W*hether it was the tears she shed on his behalf or the way she trustingly leaned against his chest and accepted his arms around her, neither was as potent as the compassion and adoration unintentionally flowing towards him. The soft, warm light of her healing magic was the beacon he'd been searching for, the balm to his battered soul he'd been without for most of his life. Just being near her cleared away the fog of confusion and allowed him to feel *almost real.*

For so long...too long, he'd been nothing more than a means to an end for a powerful evil hellbent on destroying all goodness in the universe. He possessed what they wanted, and they were prepared to do anything right up to the point of death to get the information.

But the fuckers always kept me alive. Was it worth it?

If he had a nickel for every time he'd prayed for death, he'd be a very, *very* rich man. It wasn't so much the torture or the pain, it was the not knowing that had driven him mad.

What day was it? Where were they? Was his family alive?

Had his Clan been destroyed? Had the Bitch decimated Dragon Kin?

The times he'd been forced to listen to her constant ramblings ad nauseam still made him sick...

"Give me what I want, Dragon," she hissed, running the tip of *her poison-coated talons under his chin. "You can rule by my side. Just think...a legion of Demons at your command. You'll be unstoppable."*

Digging into his battered and scarred flesh, her fetid breath assaulted his senses as she taunted, "All the other Dragons, the ones who left you with me to rot, will be cannon-fodder. Dead. Gone. You will be able to forge a new future. Have your own kingdom to rule as you see fit. Just imagine..."

Days, weeks, months, and even a couple times years passed in which they tried to trick him into revealing the Secret. They'd gone so far as to bring in a boy about his age, seventeen at the time.

For almost an entire day Sable had talked to the teenager, devoured his stories of the outside world, even played cards and drew pictures in the dirt. Then the young Dragon sensed a dramatic change in the boy. An acidic whiff of Cinquefoil, a blurring of the teenager's visage, and finally, the glittering ashes of Vervain falling from under the cuff of the boy's shirt.

Picking up the playing cards while continuing to chatter away, Sable made a show of demonstrating the trick his uncle had taught him right before he and Stone's twelfth birthday. Purposely bumbling the cards time and time again, the young Dragon used the deception to run his fingers through the Vervain then whispering the words of the Revealing Spell his *seanmhair* had taught him.

Heartbroken when his suspicions became truth, and the 'boy' morphed back into one of the Overlords, Sable spent the next six months in total isolation. His captors had seen it as a punishment, often leaving him for days without food or water, but the young Paladin was happy for the respite. Any time away from his cruel captors was well worth hunger and thirst. Herne saw to Sable's welfare as best he could even through the dense black magic, they used to keep him from communicating with his Clan...and his twin.

Unfortunately, it all ended much too soon...

The sounds of Lore's whispered sobs drew his attention, blessedly pulled him from the horror of his memories. Inhaling her scent, letting it fill every fiber of his being with a peace he'd never known, Sable lowered the remaining shields in his mind. He would give her a chance to explore on her own, to ask questions, seek out the person he truly was before pushing the information he, and he alone, had carried since his birth into his Mate's mind.

It had to be done. He could no longer be trusted to keep it safe. The only thing anchoring him to this reality, keeping whatever sanity he could muster in the forefront of his fractured psyche was the tiny, dark-haired woman before him.

Unable to hold back, needing to be utterly honest with the woman the Universe made for him, Sable kissed the top of his Tigress' head before whispering, "Please don't cry. I don't deserve your tears."

Turning in his arms, her face a mask of sorrow and confusion, Lore narrowed her eyes, causing an unshed tear to cascade down her cheek as she asked, "How can you say that? I've seen your scars." She laid her hand over his heart. "I can feel your pain. You didn't do this shit to yourself."

Holding back a metric ton of self-hatred and recrimination with only a thin, fraying rope of magical hope, he could only pray his lucidity wouldn't sleep as he shook with the effort and tried not to snarl. "Because I went with *them* willingly."

Pushing out of his arms and taking a step backward, her expression changed in a single beat of his heart. Gone was the tearful woman who had been mourning what had been done to her Mate, and in her place appeared the logical, analytic doctor with a sharp wit and need to know every detail. Seeing the questions springing to life in her mind, it still shocked him at how quickly she started firing them in his direction.

"Who are you talking about? When did this happen? Were 'they' the ones who hurt you? How long were you with 'them'?" Taking a breath so quickly he couldn't get a word in, she went on, "And while we're at it. Why did you attack your brother? Your twin? Do you know Jewel? How do you know Jewel? Why the fuck would Annika break into my Clinic? We've been friends forever. Was it your brother's idea? Why would she go along with it? Why would he attack you? Me? Doesn't he know what you've been through? What the..."

"Stop!" The roar was out of his mouth and bouncing around the grotto like a runaway rubber ball before he'd been able to stop it.

Reaching for her, he felt the slap of not only her magic but also her temper as Lore took a giant step backward, shook her head and raised her hands as if to push him away before snarling, "And that's enough of that bullshit. You don't scare me." Reversing her motion with the dignity and grace of the true Queen of her Pride, the one she should have been - would have been - had all of her kin not been slaughtered by Hunters and her parents not taken by some genetically-engineered disease she'd yet to identify, the tip of her index finger ground into his chest. "This can go one of two ways. I can help you, or I can kick your ass. The choice is yours."

Swamped in guilt and embarrassment, searching for the right words to express the depth of his remorse, the icy claws of the demons of the past latched onto his mind. For so long, he'd been drowning in the pain he'd caused Stone. Had been unable to answer his twin's calls. Been held hostage by the look of betrayal in his brother's eyes as he'd willingly ridden off with the enemy.

But I didn't know. I really didn't know...

It had taken nearly a decade of meditation and communion with his Dragon King to block the bond he shared with Stone. *"Be cannie whit ye wish fur, mah laddie,"* Herne had advised. *"The union ye shaur wi' yer twin isnae tae be broken."*

And the Dragon King had been right. Not his tormentors' whips, fiery pokers, or silver chains had hurt nearly as much as the severing of his link to Stone. Over time, he'd filled the hole left in his heart with hatred for the Overlords, all the while promising *never* to unleash it on anyone but them. How could he have let it hurt the one person in the world he was meant to protect?

All but falling onto the bench he and his twin had built from driftwood and rocks when they were still young and innocent, Sable kept his eyes glued to Lore's. Opening his mouth, trying to speak, he coughed and sputtered, but no words ever came. Lodged in his throat, wedged so tightly it was hard to breathe, every syllable became his enemy.

And then they came...

Ragged talons atop skeletal hands closed around his throat. Thick silver bands clamped tight around his chest. Rattling chains and mocking taunts filled his ears. The crack of the whip, the tearing of flesh, the scent of his own skin burning as they branded him with ancient demonic runes invaded his senses, but one word still echoed in his mind...

"Lore."

"Yes. Yes. It's me. What's wrong...?"

So far away, little more than a whisper, her words carried such emotion, such power, but they couldn't be real. They were a product of his wishful thinking just as they'd been so many other times.

No! She was real. Had to be authentic. He'd been in the ice. Had prayed for death. But she'd saved him. Hadn't she?

His mind warred with itself. What was reality? What was a nightmare?

Had the petite woman with long dark hair, deep brown eyes, and touch so caring she'd made him believe in a future outside captivity been a living, breathing person, or a construct of his mind to avoid his own harsh existence? Did the Overlords trick him again? Create her from some horrific spell to take the last bit of his humanity, his sanity, his life?

She had to have been a dream. Only one woman ever came to his prison, and she was a pure evil that haunted the bravest men's nightmares.

Forged in the depths of Hell by Lilith herself to be the handmaiden to the Queen of the Damned. She took pleasure in other's pain, ate the souls of her victims for fun, and swallowed their last breaths to celebrate her victory.

The Overlords sent for *her* when they truly wanted to make Sable feel inescapable, eternal agony. The Witch could bring him to death's door, steal the beat from his heart, let the Reaper's scythe chip away at his soul, then leave him dangling on the edge of his own personal Hell for weeks on end.

Was she here? Had they called her? What had he done this time?

No! I'm not there anymore. I'm free. In the cave where Stone and I played. Aren't I? Aren't I? "Aren't I?"

"Aren't you what? Sable? Sable, talk to me? Aren't you what?"

Her voice sounded frantic. There was genuine pain, genuine fear, an undeniable need to help in her tone. And... love... Could it be?

"Why, ...ar-are...y-you...?" Unable to finish. Fighting against the suffocating fingers around his neck, he gulped at the thinning air.

"Why am I what?" She was screaming now. Why was she

screaming if she didn't care? If she was the one inflicting so much pain?

"Because she isn't." Herne's voice was muffled. What was wrong with the Dragon King? Was it really him or another trick of Sable's fractured mind?

"I hope like hell this doesn't hurt, but I don't know another way to find out what is wrong." Her voice was filled with tenderness and regret. What was she going to do? Why was she apologizing? She was already killing him.

No! It's not her! The inner struggle, the arguing within his own mind, was relentless. There had to be a way to figure out what was real and what was...

Metaphysical fingers probed his mind. It was a gentle examination. Not the poking, stabbing, prodding invasion he'd endured so very many times.

It couldn't be the Overlords. No way it was the Witch. No one who'd come to his cave had ever been as tender.

"Are you..." Words cut off by his own anguished cries as hot pokers battered his mental shields and attacked his consciousness. He had to do something...*anything.*

Reaching for Lore, he put all his faith in the honest, innocent strength he prayed was really his Mate. But it was too late. He'd waited too long. Shoving his head between his legs, Sable gasped for air as he prayed for death.

Bile burnt his esophagus and filled his mouth. Gagging and retching with such violence, he fell forward, the next sound he heard was the crushing of the bones in his nose as his face slammed into the stone floor.

"Son of a bitch!" Lore's curse was more of a pained snarl, her regret palpable as she added, "Why the fuck did I let that happen?"

She was real! Had to be real. No one had ever given a shit if his bones were broken. In fact, they'd laughed and hit him harder. Even wiped his blood on their faces like some sick badge of honor.

Rearing its ugly head, Doubt chuckled sardonically in the deep recesses of his mind, *"It's another trick, Asshole. No one loves you. No one cares about you. Why don't you just die and make life easier for all of us."*

"Fuck you!" He roared in return, grinning through the pain as Lore snarled, "You better be talking to the voices in your head, Dragon."

"Fuck you, too!" He sneered again, the words little more than garbled grunts and wispy wheezes.

Caught between fact and fiction, reality and psychosis, one thing remained, he had to escape. Had to hide. Had to find a way to piece whatever was left of his mind back together. He couldn't be retaken.

Digging his fingers into the granite, ignoring the pain of the skin being ripped, he struggled to pull his heaving body away from the only good thing he knew. It didn't matter if she was fact or fiction, she was **his** and the bastards could not and would never be allowed to use her against him.

"Mother Fuc..." Her words trailed off, turning into a low, threatening growl that emanated down her arm and into her hand on his shoulder before vibrating through his body. "What the fuck did they do to you?" She spat the question as a threat towards the Overlords.

Was it her in his mind? If so, then she had to real, right? But still... What was she looking for? Why didn't she ask? What was...

"There it is!" She sounded happy, almost triumphant, and more determined if that was possible. It made him feel good to know he'd helped even if he had no clue how.

Swept away in another tsunamic wave of pain, the thump of boot heels against rock filled his ears. The dank stench of sweaty leather combined with the acerbic reek of evil sorcery assaulted his senses.

They were coming. There was no denying it. They'd found him or had he never been free of them? Whatever the case, Lore, if she was real, had to leave. He had to make her go.

"Stop it," she demanded, slapping at his hands as he tried to push her off while grabbing the waistband of his pants with her free hand. "I'm getting us out of here. You really don't get a vote, Dragon Man."

What had she said? Where were they going? How could she get him past the Overlords? What about...?

"Hold on, Dragon..."

Her words cut through his frenzied thoughts only to immediately fade into the distance. She was real. Had to be. There was no other explanation. But did that mean the Overlords were real, too? Was he real?

Opening his mouth, whatever he was about to say was completely swallowed up in a massive swell of barely contained, completely wild Feline magic. Was she...? Could she...?

All his unvoiced questions were answered when Lore's hands grabbed his bound ones at the same time that she announced, "Up, up, and away. Hold onto your ass. I have no fuckin' clue how to drive this thing, and the manual in your brain is a pile of jumbled horse crap."

CHAPTER ELEVEN

"Shit. Shit. Shitshitshitshitshit! What the hell am I doing?" Yes, she was unashamedly shrieking at herself. It was the only thing keeping her upright and sane. Talking to the unconscious Dragon, she answered her own question, "I'm getting you back to my Clinic before you croak on me. That's what I'm doing, *dammit*. And no, talking to myself does not make me nuckin' futs. Neither does answering my own questions." Side-eyeing the Paladin, she added, "And yes, I know that Dragon's don't croak, and you can't answer. So, that's making the fact that I'm talking to myself your fault." Forcing herself to smile, she added with a chuckle, "That's my story, and I'm stickin' to it."

Well aware she was stalling with the hopes that Sable would wake up and take over, Lore once again cursed, "Oh fuck it! Dad always said I would die trying something stupid that I had no business doing. He was probably right. Always was. Here's hoping I don't take you with me, Dragon Man." Giving a mock salute to the air around her, still wondering who or what the blasted Dragon was crawling away from when he collapsed, she chirped with a heavy dose of cynicism, "Here's to you, Pops."

Wearing the damn-near seven-foot tall Dragon over her shoulders like he was a monogrammed cardigan and she was a preppy socialite headed to the docks for a party on Muffy's or Buffy's or Puffy's yacht, Lore shoved her magic down the same metaphysical highway she'd plucked from Sable's mind. Praying to every deity she could think of, and a few she made up along the way, she continued the flow of magic into what felt like a bottomless well.

For one incredibly long second, absolutely nothing happened. Holding her breath, sure she'd failed, and Sable was going to die in her arms, she cursed under her breath as she tried to come up with plan B.

Then all hell broke loose in the best possible way that hell can ever break loose. In less time than it takes for an eye to blink, she and her backpack-in-the-shape-of-a-huge-Dragon-Shifter were whizzing through time and space.

"Son of a bitch!" She cheered right along with the happy roaring of her Tigress.

Refusing to be beaten, knowing she'd never live it down when Minka found out what a baby she'd been, Lore grabbed hold of her magic with an iron grip and centered her mind. Gripping Sable's hands so tightly that the blunt tips of her nails dug into the flesh of his wrists, everything instantly became clear...well, as clear as flying faster than the speed of light through a hole in the fabric of the universe can be. All she had to do was think about where she wanted to be and trust in the Universe's infinite wisdom.

Looking straight ahead while following the path in the Dragon's mind, she realized with only a split-second to spare that they were about to zoom right past the Arctic Circle, Baffin Island, her own little piece of paradise, and end up somewhere close to Santa's Workshop in the off-season. Using Sable's bound hands like the controller on her PlayStation, another thing she prayed he wouldn't remember, Lore made a seriously abrupt, scarily sharp, and neck-breaking right turn, then pointed her mystical vision squarely at her Clinic.

Holding her breath, keeping the image of the largest Triage room in the forefront of her mind, she knew the exact second they'd passed from what she would always think of as 'Sable's Space-Time Continuum' to the purely magical realm then through the very hard, very real walls of her home without so much as breaking a sweat. It was in that very moment, it dawned on her that she had no idea how to stop once her feet hit the ground and did the only thing she could think of, yelled her fool head off.

"Watch out below if anyone's down there! I don't know how to stop this crazy thing! You've been warned. If I run over you, you can't sue. Won't get shit anyway."

The sound of Jewel's chuckle was nothing short of the voice of an angel as the Nymph assured, "Ah got ye, mah lass."

Just like a warm hug, a favorite blanket, and a kiss from mom all wrapped up into one, Jewel's magic wrapped around Lore and her passenger. Letting go of the white-knuckled grip she had on the mash-up of her magic and Sable's, Lore happily and gratefully allowed the Nymph to bring them down safely... but that was as far as her good nature lasted.

No sooner had the soles of her boots hit the floor than she took in the cast of characters, including a few new ones, and immediately hissed, "Stand the fuck back. This is all your fault."

"But..."

Jabbing her finger towards Stone, she growled, "Stand. The. Fuck. Back."

"Do as she says, Stone," the most prominent of the newcomers ordered. Tall, with an air of command and piercing silver eyes, the Paladin took a single step forward. Smiling, something she could tell he didn't do very often, the General, as she'd instantly named him, calmly introduced, "Miss Bransfield, my name is Creed Mathers. If it helps, I knew your father."

"Nope, doesn't."

With the rise of a single eyebrow and the clearing of his throat, the General continued as if she hadn't said anything. "I apologize for the intrusion, but the Dragon King with whom Sable shares his soul called for us." Taking another, more confident step forward, he went on, "This is unprecedented among our kind." Deludedly thinking he'd won her over, he relaxed his straight-backed, barely-at-ease, too-many-years-in-'the service', stick-up-his-ass stance, and added with an obligatory snicker, "So, we came without an invitation."

Done listening, even though she could see he wanted to go on, Lore held up her hand and interrupted, "I'll get to you in a minute... Gener...I mean, ummm..."

"Creed," he reminded.

"Yeah, that," she dismissed, eyes already on Annika. Pointing at the Vixen as if her thumb and forefinger were a gun, Lore scoffed, "What's the deal, Dude? Why the fuck did you and your *Dragon*," she spat the word like it tasted bad because in Stone's case it did, "break into my place like you were auditioning for Tom Cruise's part in Mission Impossible 25?" Slapping her hand against the side of her leg, she huffed, "You forgot how to ring the bell? Knock on the damned door? Make a fucking call? Send a friggin' smoke signal?"

"She didn't..."

"Shut up, Stone. Just shut the ever-loving hell right the duck-in-a-puddle up," she snarled at the Dragon. "I was talking to Annika. I know her. I like her. I *trusted* her. You, I do not know. Damn sure, do not like. And wouldn't trust you any farther than I could pick you up and throw you." Taking a breath as she realized she was still holding Sable on her back and should already be examining him instead of interrogating her 'visitors,' she added, "Which, by the way, would be about a quarter mile. So, do the math, Asshole. You're not shit or the stick in my book." Giving Stone an extra bitchy glare, she added in a low, threatening tone, "Now, I'm gonna save your twin's life, and you can go straight to hell."

Sure there was a story there, something she should've checked out before she went all cat-shit-crazy and yelled at the Dragon-on-her-back's twin, Lore decided not to ask questions, but instead get the details from Sable's mind. "Easier, more efficient, and with no extraneous bullshit. Just the way I like it," she mumbled to herself.

The chuckle of the blond-haired, blue-eyed, Viking-looking Dragon at the back of the group made her like him before being introduced, but she wasn't about to give up that information. The whole blasted lot of them were on her shit list, something she'd deal with later. At that moment, making sure Sable was okay was the *only thing* that mattered.

Turning towards the double doors of the enormous Triage she kept set up and ready for injured predators, Lore made it exactly two steps before the sound of footsteps behind her made her stop dead in her tracks. Without looking backward, she ground out through gritted teeth, "Stop where you are. Do not even *think about* following me. I'm gonna take care of whatever is happening to Sable...*alone*." Snapping her head to the side, she glared at every single person in attendance before adding, "If you do decide you know better than me or can get the jump on me, I'll have Jewel zap all your asses to the tiniest iceberg in the middle of the Arctic Ocean. Ya' get me?" Not waiting for an answer, she added, "Jewel, I'm gonna need your help, and where the hell is Minka?"

Thankful Annika and the Dragons took her at her word and stayed put, allowing Lore to make quick work of getting

Sable onto the gurney. Still pissed at Jewel and needing to know precisely what her connection to the Paladin was but knowing she would need the Nymph's help, Lore pushed everything but Sable to the back of her mind and instructed, "We need to scan him. Something's in there." Pointing to his chest, she added, "Something nasty bad that's trying to worm its way out through his brain."

"Aye," Jewel answered, the crack in her voice stopping Lore mid-turn.

"Are you crying?"

"No, no, just a touch of a cold."

"Yeah, and I gotta touch of the fleas." Continuing to turn and grabbing a surgical gown and scrubs, she started undressing without missing a beat. "You might as well give it up, 'cause when I know Sable's outta trouble, I'm gonna grill your ass like a burger on Independence Day. You lied to me. Don't even try to deny it. I don't know why, or what the hell you hoped to gain, but I know damn good and well that you did and that pisses me off almost as bad as what's been done to him."

Feeling like fire ants were crawling up her legs and down her arms from the spike of tension in the room, she thought about smoothing things over, but instead snapped, "And cut that shit out. You know the stench of guilt makes me gag. You fucked up. You know you did. If it was for a good reason, we'll fix it. If it wasn't, you can get the fuck out."

"Aye," was the only response she got from the Nymph and quite frankly, the only one she needed.

If she found out Jewel had anything at all to do with what was happening to Sable, Lore would rip her limb from limb and leave her remains out in the cold. It was as simple as that.

Locking everything but the Dragon in front of her and the need to make him happy, healthy, and whole in one of the millions of compartments in her brain, she reached for the handle on the camera of the portable x-ray camera. It dawned on her that she should probably put on a lead apron, but then Sable let out an ear-splitting, keening wail and she moved as quickly as she possibly could.

Watching as the images flashed on the plain white wall across the room, she looked for any anomaly, injury, or foreign object that could be poisoning the Paladin. Lost in thought, trying to come up with any possible explanation besides the one staring her in the face, Lore nearly jumped out of her skin when one of the huge metal swinging doors creaked open.

Glaring at the chiseled features of the Viking, she snapped, "Get the fuck out!"

Ignoring her warning, he entered with his hands up in surrender. Smiling a smile Lore knew had made more than one woman drop her knickers and beg to be screwed, he quickly explained, "Name's Gunnar. Been a Healer for centuries and a medical doctor for decades. Maybe I can help."

"Yeah, sure, whatever," she reluctantly relented, glaring at Jewel when she dared to snicker.

"Nice set up you have here," the Viking commented, clearly trying to make small talk as he made his way across the room and took Jewel's place on the opposite side of Sable. With his back to Lore, he pointed at the images on the wall. "Everything looks normal."

"Yeah, except for all the evidence of broken and rebroken bones, battered organs, and contusions so deep they had to have been made with silver."

"Mmhmm," he mumbled, walking closer to the wall. Turning so quickly he was little more than a blur, Gunnar snapped his fingers and confirmed, "But it's not silver poisoning."

"No shit, Sherlock," she groused. "I cleared all that shit outta his system first thing. Not my first rodeo."

Deciding to ignore the Dragon Doctor and do what she did best, Lore opted to take a nonconventional, incredibly magical approach to diagnose whatever was trying to destroy Sable. Laying her right palm on his throat and her left over his heart, she let her eyes slide shut, and her mind's eye delve inside the Paladin's body.

Wading through wave after wave of living embodiment of decade after decade of mental, physical, emotional abuse...the scars of what had been inflicted upon Sable, she instantly felt the presence of another. Reinforcing the magical shields, she always carried at the same time that she extended them to the Paladin, she edged closer and closer to the malevolent presence.

Following her Tigress' lead, together they stalked their prey. Weaving in and around the mystical roadblocks Sable had constructed, his own personal security system, the long, dark, misshapen shadow of the interloper came into view. Squatting like a fat, wart-covered toad just waiting for Sable to fuck up and reveal whatever it wanted, the trespasser stunk of black magic and sulfur.

"Demon" floated through her mind but was quickly replaced by Witch. No sooner had the word flashed into view than so did *she*.

Standing up in one fluidly graceful, incredibly intimidating move, the Witch's visage remained in the shadows. Needing to confront the bitch, exorcise her from Sable's being and banish her back to the Pits of Hell, Lore readied herself to attack.

"NO!" Sable roared. "No! No! NoNoNo! You will not take her!"

Thrown out of his body and across the room, Lore's ass hit the floor right before her head bounced off the concrete wall. Seeing stars but still trying to get to her feet, she made it as far as her knees before Sable jumped off the table, conjured his sword from empty air, and began fighting an imaginary enemy, all the while screaming in Gaelic, that she suddenly understood as if it was her native tongue, "No more, Malvolia! No more! You'll never get what you want!"

Throwing his blade into the air where it instantly disappeared as he conjured up one helluva big hunting knife with the opposite hand, Sable swung the blade towards his own neck and declared, "It ends here!"

Watching in horror, unable to move fast enough while screaming, "Stop" at the top of her lungs, Lore nearly fainted when Gunnar appeared at Sable's side. Touching the first two fingers of his left hand to Sable's forehead, the Viking whispered, "*Cadal.*"

Looking at Lore as he caught the suddenly unconscious Sable, the Viking grinned, "Well, you found the 'problem.' Any idea how to *kill* her and keep our boy alive?"

CHAPTER TWELVE

"*S*he'll not be savin' you, Dragon."

Was she real this time? Really there? Or was the Witch a figment of his warped imagination?

"Oh, I'm real, you little piece of horse shite. And I'm 'bout ta make ya' burn." Her thick East Ender accent and the accompanying hiss reminded him of the children's fable about the snake parading as a lamb.

Sliding the tip of her black, ragged nail under his pectoral muscle before grounding it into his sternum with such force he could hear the bone splintering, she cackled so loudly he thought his ears might burst. *"I told ya' I'd make it hurt when I finally got tae kill ya'. You're the only one ta ever defy me. Ta ever escape with his hide intact."*

"My hide intact?" He wheezed. *"You skinned me more times than I can remember."*

"But ya' always grew it back. Blasted Dragon magic!"

Sliding her skeletal fingers under his rib cage and around his heart, she clutched his heart and squeezed so hard the blood screeched to a grinding, agonizing halt in his veins. Caught in the endless web of her black magic and pure wickedness, he was the fly and she the spider, entirely at the Witch's mercy, unable to move or cry out, only listen to Lore screaming orders and feel the anguish his pain caused his Mate.

"Grab the crash cart!"

"Fuck that!" A deep male voice he recognized as Gunnar Brask, a real blast from a very distant past, yelled back. "Everybody's hands on Sable. NOW!"

Bombarded by a superfluity of magic the size of Mt Rushmore with eight extra presidents, he felt his back bow off the table as the powerful muscle of his heart viciously fought against the Witch's magical grip. Again, and again, they zapped him with magic. Over and over, the wretched bitch chortled at their defeat.

"No one can best me, Boy. This time I came prepared. Ya' shoulda just told me what I wanted to know, and this would all be over."

Flooded with a blanket of unholy mysticism that ate at every fiber of his being, Sable struggled to stay lucid. *"An- and s-so...so would all life on – on ear-earth,"* he stammered, needing to fight back no matter how weak he became.

"No time to be a hero, Dragon Dearie."

"It's not working!"

Lore's desperate cry cut him to the quick. He didn't deserve her grief, her pity...anything from her. If she knew the truth, the whole truth, she would see saving him was a waste of her time and energy. She would know that...

"Oh, boohoo," the Witch taunted, closing her fist even tighter. *"Poor little Dragon Boy, still can't fight his own battles."* Her mind's eye meeting his, the black of her soulless gaze beat at the mental walls he'd built around the *Rún Naofa*, she hissed, *"Tell me what I want to know, and I kill ya' quick. Keep fighting me, and I'll keep you alive for centuries and bathe in your blood."*

"Stand back!"

Was that Jewel? What was she doing here? Had she always been here? Had he seen her? Was she...?

"Give me yer hands, Lass, an' grab Stone's an' Annika's!"

It was Jewel! There was no way she was a hallucination. He'd know his old nanny's voice anywhere, wouldn't he? If only he could...

Once again blasted off the table by a tidal wave of magic, when his body landed back on the gurney, he was finally blessedly alone. Light-headed, barely able to breathe, his felt Herne spring to life, forcing his heart to beat and his blood to flow.

A spark of electricity skittered up his arm, through his still-stuttering heart and straight to his soul when Lore's fingers rested on his wrist. If only there were more time, but it was a luxury he didn't have.

No one knew better than him that the Witch was never far, just hiding out, regrouping, and planning her next attack. One he feared she might just win.

Forcing his eyes open as he rolled his hand over and slid his fingers through Lore's, he whispered, "N-Need to ta – ta-talk."

"How the holy-Hades-in-seal-skin-*kamiks* are you up?" Her words drifted on a sharp exhale of complete and utter shock. Ignoring the round-robin of hoots and hollers she'd started, Lore continued holding onto the calm, relaxed demeanor that decades as not only a Tigress but a specialist in veterinary trauma had given her, "How are you awake? Alive? Breathing?" Looking around the room for answers then right back at him when she got none, the Tigress added, "Are you sure you're ready to talk?"

"Don't look a gift horse in the mouth, Lore. He's back. That's all that matters," Stone chuckled, appearing on the opposite side of the bed.

Lifting his hand, Sable gripped his twin with what little

strength he had. It was a miracle, a dream come to true, to be alive and in the same room as the brother he'd lost so very long ago. It was also good to meet Stone's Mate, the mystical Arctisune.

Then came Creed, a man Sable had only known as 'dad's friend' when he'd been kidnapped and then Gunnar - the Viking they'd trained alongside, all grown up and looking very much the spitting image of his own father. Winking at Minka, vaguely remembering the playful way she and Lore had argued as they tried to find him when he'd first arrived, he breathed a sigh of relief when the Snow Leopard gave him a nod and half a smile. Finally, his eyes landed on Jewel, the Nymph who'd been his nanny, his second mother, and the woman who explained sex to him and Stone when everyone else refused.

Tears streaming down her face, the tips of her pointed ears twinkling with starlight, and her usually lavender hair a bright pink that lit up the entire room, she moved Stone out of the way and jumped up on the bed beside him. Leaning over and kissing his cheek, she whispered, "Ah ne'er gae up on ye, mah Lad an' Ah ne'er will." Kissing him again, she added, "Troost yer Mate, me boy. She's a keeper, oone af th' guid ones. She'll understand an' loove ye mair in spite af everythin'."

Feeling Lore watching them and the ticking clock racing towards the Witch's inevitable return, Sable nodded at his old nanny and let out the breath he'd been holding. Refusing to let go of his Mate's hand even when she tried to pull away, he shoved his pain away and forced his aching body to sit up.

Looking around the room, he hoped his smile reached his eyes as he was forced to clear his throat twice and accept some ice chips from Lore to get out more than a heavy croaking sound. Working hard to speak without sounding like a frog, his eyes met hers as he humbly stated, "I really need to speak with my Mate. I promise to talk to everyone as soon as I've had time to explain a few things to her."

Trying not to burst out laughing as Lore's eyes got the size of saucers and turned the brilliant blue of her Tigress, he lost the battle when she yelped, "The fuck you say? Mate? Now, I know you've lost your damn mind."

CHAPTER THIRTEEN

*I*t was bad enough he'd announced to a room full of people, most of whom she'd just met, that she was his Mate, but now the delusional, deranged, and downright crazy-banana-pants Dragon wanted her to believe he had something called the *Rún Naofa* buried in his brain. A Truth so mystical, magical, and all-encompassing that it held the key to *absolutely everything*. And, as if that wasn't crazy enough, the fate of not only the known world but the whole oh-my-Goddess-in-a-tube-top universe depended on Sable keeping it out of the hands of the Overlords and their Head Bitch in Charge ~ the Witch.

"And you want to give me this secret...I mean *Rún Naofa?*" Feeling the need to pace, or maybe get furry and rip the stuffing out of a couch or two, she started to walk while continuing. "And, since this 'secret' can never be spoken aloud, you have to mentally 'slide' it to me. But we're gonna have to do it in a super-spy-sneaky-down-low-in-the-vault kinda way because the Witch is quite literally squatting in your brain." Making air quotes, which any other time she absolutely hated, Lore made a quick U-turn to avoid running headlong into a wall and went right on talking. "And... here's the kicker, as if everything else wasn't ball-busting-mind-blowing - you have no idea what this secret or truth is because it is so powerful your mind, or mine as the case just might be, would melt or implode or cease to function because of the vastness of the information. Only that the guy who was the Bearer ahead of you who died..."

"Was killed."

"Oh yeah, right. Killed by the Witch who is squatting inside of you..."

"Metaphysically speaking."

"Metaphysically died? Or metaphysically squatting inside of you?"

"He died the true death. She is metaphysically squatting, as you put it, inside of me."

"Yeah, okay. That's what I thought." She took a quick breath. "And this happened right before you and Stone turned...umm...

"Thirteen," he jumped in when she couldn't remember then added more. "Actually, the day before. This is significant because that is when a Dragon Shifter meant to be a Guards-man, or in our case, a Paladin, receive their Blessing from the Elders and the Ancients."

"Yeah, yeah, yeah," she got right back into her reiteration, needing to make sure she understood his gibberish while figuring out if he had hitched a ride on the Good Ship Lollipop *and* if she was going to buy a ticket, too. "So, my question right here is, why do you have to give the Da-Doo-Run-Run..."

"Rún Naofa." He smiled, making her heart do a big old flip-flop then pitter-pat. Her reaction to the stupid Dragon was both joyful and scary as hell and something she planned to ignore for as long as she could.

"I promise, I'll get it next time." She started pacing again.

"So, like I was saying, why do you have to give me the Secret Truth if Stone has it buried in his soul, too? Can't he just carry the 'torch' for a while? Goddess knows you've suffered enough. It's his turn to keep up his side of this twinship, don'tcha think?"

No longer looking her in the eye, in fact, looking everywhere *but* at her, Sable stammered and stuttered then drank a full glass of water, cleared his throat and coughed a couple of times before finally letting out a sharp exhale and meeting her gaze. "Ya' see, the morning before our Blessing, I went looking for dad and found him talking to the Elder. No, I shouldn't have been eavesdropping. Hell, I wasn't even supposed to be anywhere near the Crystal Caves, but I really thought whatever I needed to ask my father couldn't wait."

"It's called being a teenager," she teased, needing to ease his mounting anxiety. Her growing feelings for the crazy Dragon were scary, to say the least, but undeniable in a bone-deep, cellular, all-the-way-to-her-soul kinda way. Admitting he was her Mate was inevitable. She knew it. Her Tigress knew it. The problem was, speaking the words aloud made it real, and that was something that terrified Lore to the very tippy-tip of her striped tail.

Turning her full attention back to Sable as he nodded. She noted his skin slowly returning to the soft gray pallor it had been before he'd awakened. It had to be the Witch. She was draining him, sucking the life out of him, all just to get that blasted fucking secret. If Lore ever got a chance, she'd rip that nasty bitch's head off. But first, she needed to listen and learn and decide what to do.

Taking another deep breath, Sable continued with a sad chuckle, "Yeah, you're probably right, not that I know much about being a teenager." Another heavy sigh and he added, "Anyway, I overheard them discussing the *Rún Naofa*. So, of course, I hunkered down and listened to every word. The Elder's explanation was unlike anything I'd ever heard before. He said because we were twins, we would both receive our Blessings at the same time so that the *Rún Naofa* would be split equally between us."

"Well, Dad wasn't having any part of that. The old man was adamant that when the Ancients called to him before we were born, the agreement was for only one of his sons to be the Bearer. It was a known fact that the Bearer would leave the Clan when the time was right, but there was no way he was giving up both of us."

"Their argument went on for what seemed like forever and then Carrick, one of the oldest of all Dragon Kin..."

"Carrick? Like Carrick Carrick?" She blurted out, not believing her ears. "Tall guy, salt and pepper hair, blue eyes, a wicked sense of humor and a serious problem with knowing absolutely everything?" Her hands were flying all over the place, adding to her description and her excitement. Finally, there was something she understood! But the Dragon in front of her had a much different reaction.

"Yeah, that's him," Sable growled, his pupils elongating to that of his Dragon's as sparkling granite scales superimposed over his skin. "How do *you* know *him*?"

"Dude, you seriously have to control your green-eyed monster."

"You're my Ma..."

"Don't say *that* word. We'll deal with that after the Wicked Witch is a puddle of goo, and you're healthy."

Holding up her index finger as he opened his mouth to interrupt, she realized it was a waste of time to try to shut him up. Because of their 'connection,' she could hear every damn thing he was thinking, and the guy was broadcasting his thoughts so loudly he might as well have hired a plane and had them written in the sky for all to see. But Lore loved a challenge, and so she started countering his high-handed, Alpha-male, unspoken egotism.

"I know your Dragon doesn't have green eyes. I was calling you jealous, Butthead. And you need to cool it, whatever we are to each other, it appears that we're gonna need some ground rules, 'cause I don't do macho assholes, no matter how cute they are or how many times I save their lives."

Grabbing his hand so he would chill out because his breathing was getting shallower and his skin a darker shade of gray, also so he could feel the honesty of her words as well as hear it, she added, "And, the most important thing you should've waited for me to say is that Carrick is my Godfather."

Sufficiently repentant, he sheepishly grinned before chuckling, "Oh, me and my big mouth."

"And huge ego," she giggled. "So, now that that's all cleared up continue, please. Cause I'm only gonna let this explanation go on a little longer. You are looking really worse for wear. You need an IV and lots of rest. Don't you guys have a Healing Sleep you can go into? I swear, I remember that from some class or another."

"We do, but I can't."

Grumbling under her breath when he used her own move against her and held up his index finger, Lore gave a begrudging nod.

"So, Carrick walked in, asked what was going on, and after hearing both sides of the disagreement said only one twin had to carry the *Rún Naofa* and that it would be the one who first received his Blessing. Dad quickly spoke up, stating since we were destined to be Paladin, he wanted Stone to be the Bearer, and as the oldest son, I would go on to carry our legacy within the Clan and the Paladin Force."

"But..." She prompted when he took a little too long to continue.

"But I had done my research. I knew *what* being the Bearer meant. I knew whoever carried the *Rún Naofa* would leave home sooner rather than later. Would be on the run or in hiding for most of his life. A life that would be spent alone, something my brother hated."

Feeling the pregnant pause, waiting for Sable to continue, Lore couldn't take the suspense for longer than a minute and urged with a healthy dose of humor to lift the dour mood in the room, "So, ya' gonna leave me hangin'? You *have* to finish. It's really uncool to stop at the climax of the story."

Shaking his head, looking like he'd lost his favorite baseball card, dropped his ice cream cone, and his dog had run away, Sable solemnly admitted, "Stone and I are known as the Twin Flames - one to guard the past while the other forges the future. Being the firstborn, I was always meant to guard the past..."

"And Stone was always meant to forge the future."

"Right. So, if I let him receive his Blessing first, I was dooming him to live a life he wasn't meant for."

"Okay, I see where you're coming from, but that still doesn't explain what you started to tell me in the cave. Why don't you think you're worth being saved?"

"Because I knew someone was coming for me, or more to the point, for the *Rún Naofa*. I also heard Carrick say the Oracles were worried about the growing numbers of Overlords. He said they were forming armies. Organizing, actually getting a battle plan together. The Oracles plan was to bring the Bearer to their Citadel. After our Blessing, when the dark clouds rolled in, I thought it was them."

Watching as tears filled his eyes, Lore grabbed his hand and held on tight, lending him the strength she hoped would help

JULIA MILLS

him continue, but true to form since the day she'd dug him out of the snow, the shit hit the fan. Falling backward, arms flailing, body shaking, and his back arching off the gurney, Sable's eyes rolled back in his head and his mouth opened in a silent scream.

He looked as if something or someone was trying to pull the skeleton from his body. Stretched in every direction, skin stretched as tight as it could go, every single bone was visible.

"That fucking bitch!" Lore roared.

Climbing up on the cot, straddling his chest, she held his body stable with her own and his head steady to keep his neck from breaking as she screamed for help. Shouting instructions to everyone who funneled into the room, she had never been so glad to see Gunnar in the lead. Unfortunately, it looked like not even the Viking was going to be enough.

Shifting her eyes back at Sable, it wasn't the soft hazel gaze of her Dragon, but the face of pure evil looking back at her. Hurling her upward, the Witch slammed the Tigress against the ceiling and let her freefall before bringing her to a jerking halt and suspending her in midair over Sable's still seizing body.

A tidal wave of the vilest, most depraved sorcery Lore had ever been subjected to filled the room instantly freezing everyone but she and Sable in place. Cackling like the true bitch from hell she was, the Sorceress taunted, "Time for fun and games, kiddies. This one's called, let's skin the cat."

CHAPTER FOURTEEN

"*I'd hate for you to miss all the fun,*" the Witch chortled. Snapping her fingers, his eyes flew open. Instantly enraged, he fought her magical shackles with every ounce of strength he could muster, pulling what little enchantment he could from his mystically-caged Dragon King.

Making a show of opening her gruesome eyes as wide as she could, the layers of crow's feet and wrinkles unfolding like the ribs of one of the fancy handheld fans all the females carried on special occasions when he was a child and hanging off her emaciated skull as she taunted him with her mock surprise. "*Oh, lookie there. Ya' do have a wee bit of fight left in ya.'*"

Leaning closer, the mangled, pock-marked skin of her sagging cheeks looked even more hideous through the distortion of his mind's eye, she whispered, "*But can ya' save your little lovely before I rip the last of her silky-smooth skin from her bones? And before I wear it as me own?*" Fetid breath assaulted his nose as she added with a ghastly wheezing chuckle, "*Or will ya' break and tell me what I want to know just to save her mangy hide?*"

Fire sparked in his veins. His body shook with a new,

unfamiliar power that perfectly blended with his own as he readily welcomed it into his heart and soul.

Looking into Lore's eyes, he could see she was preparing for a fate worse than death but refused to give Malvolia the satisfaction of tasting his Mate's fear. Unable to speak, the movement of his limbs limited to less than inches, he slammed his mental shields tight around the bond he shared with his Mate and growled, *"I'll die before she harms a hair on your head."*

"Don't worry about me. Just don't let that bitch..."

Unable to finish her statement as the Witch manifested beside her, Lore's livid gaze said it all - Kill Malvolia no matter the cost. *"Anything for you, mo chroí, but I'll not let you suffer for my crimes."*

Floating beside the suspended Lore, Malvolia sneered down at Sable, already celebrating her victory. Reaching for his Tigress' shoulder as slowly and deliberately as she could, the Witch amplified her theatrics just to taunt him, to test him...to break him.

Magic of all varieties filled the room. Sure, the Wicked Bitch of Wherever had incapacitated everyone in the room, but it didn't stop the strongest the paranormal world had to offer from trying everything in their arsenal. Sable was sure she wasn't the worst any of them had ever been up against, just the most treacherous.

Sparks ricocheted off the barrier Malvolia had constructed around Lore and herself. Thick gray smog wafted through the electrically-charged atmosphere from the miasmic combination of pure white magic and deadly dark sorcery. The others were trying their best. Unfortunately, the Witch had come prepared.

Sweat poured into Sable's eyes, drenched his chest and left puddles under his back as the ancient enchantment of his Dragon King comingled with the influx of the unfamiliar and fed the flames within him. Praying for his transformation, willing the granite scales of his beast to burst through his skin, his eyes remained trained on the Witch's finger as it mockingly inched toward Lore's shoulder.

Roaring within his own mind when the fabric of her shirt ripped open, revealing her ivory skin, his vision blurred a split-second before the jagged tip of the Witch's nail touched Lore's flesh. Sparks flew from the point of contact. The acrid stench of burning flesh filled the air, but it was the guttural snarl of her Tiger that triggered an answering roar from Herne.

The collective snarl of everyone circling his bed shook the very foundation under their feet, overshadowed only by the true ferocity and intense magnitude of the roar that blasted from the core of Sable's being. Barely noticing the scales of his Dragon ripping through his skin and his bones breaking and reforming as his transformation shredded Malvolia's magical bonds, his only focus was on saving Lore and destroying the Witch.

Leaping to his feet atop the gurney, the impenetrable armor of his Warrior Dragon covering his massive form, Sable stood over ten feet tall with his talons at the ready. Reaching for Lore, another roar flew from his lips as the Witch ripped a ribbon of skin off the crest of his Mate's shoulder to the top of her waist.

Blood sprayed in every direction covering the room in a fine mist of crimson and the scent of Lore's life essence as her Tigress roared in defiance and his Mate shook with righteous indignation still refusing to give the Witch the satisfaction of her pain. Unable to contain any semblance of control, Sable's bottom jaw dropped open, the acid from his glands mixed with the scalding heat of his fury and from one beat of his heart to the next Dragon fire bathed the mystical force-field Malvolia hid behind.

Throwing back her head, the Witch's grating guffaw resembled a nagging old mule as she impaled every single nail on her right hand into the base of Lore's neck, preparing to shred what remained of his Mate's precious skin. No longer conscious of his actions, caught up the frenzy of a Warrior pushed past the point of no return the Paladin's wings flung wide open.

Instinctually forcing the thin bones that created the framework from his wings to elongate, the already long, razor-sharp talons lining the edges grew in length and width at the same time that they curved inward creating a multitude of deadly sabers lined up and ready to rip his greatest enemy apart. Spinning with a force outside himself, everything and everyone around him was but a blur of nothingness. He'd manifested himself into a living, breathing, incredibly magical Buzzsaw and was aiming every ounce of fiery, vengeful rage at Malvolia.

The harder he pushed against the Witch's barricade, the hotter the flesh and bones of his wings became. Flashes of pure energy rebounded around the room. Burning embers of Dragon fire filled the air. He could feel her defenses weakening, but still, she crowed, "You'll not beat me, Lizard."

Doubling his resolve, pulling from the unknown magic, he refused to give in. Yes, it mattered that the scent of Lore's blood grew stronger and the white walls of the examination room were being painted red, but as long as his Mate roared, *"Don't let this fucking bitch win!"* He would follow her lead.

Incensed by her pain and rallied by her strength, his hand shot out just in time to catch his broadsword as it magically appeared. Instantly stopping his spin, he fluidly launched himself forward, the belief that he was meant to save Lore's life propelled him through the air. Crashing through the solid wall of Malvolia's sorcery, he zeroed in on the physical embodiment of all his vengeful fury.

Stopping only when his blade entered her body just under the base of her sternum, exited through her spine, and dug deep into the concrete wall at the back of the examination room, did Sable shove the shortened, scale-covered muzzle of his Warrior Dragon into her face. "Now, you die, and I plan to make it quick because the sight of you makes me sick."

Cocky as ever, a sneer on her face that showed her black, pointed teeth and gray, splotchy tongue, the Witch mocked, "Ya've not got the stones, Boy."

"But I do," a resonant voice Sable had never again expected to hear boomed.

"And I will," an otherworldly feminine voice with a steely undertone affirmed.

"Aye, will be a pleasure," the thick Scottish brogue of a Highlander bellowed.

And finally, a genuinely melodic voice with an innocence that diametrically opposed the width and breadth of its power confirmed, "Not only does he have the stones, but he also has the Blessing of the Universe."

Refusing to look away from the Witch, well aware of the treachery she could wield if given half a chance, Sable let the immense supremacy and unprecedented omnipotence being forced into his soul predicate his next action. Retracting the scales of his Dragon from his hand, he pressed his palm against Malvolia's chest.

Looking deep into her eyes, he found nothing but death and destruction, making it easy for him to calmly say, "To hell with you."

A single blessed flame of concentrated Dragon fire emanated from his palm followed by a clap of thunder and a bolt of Heavenly lightning. Enveloped in a puff a smoke, he watched the only thing left of the Witch - a smattering of worthless ash disappear into nothingness. Catching his sword as he spun in midair and dropped to the ground, Sable crossed the room at top speed.

Cutting through the aisle of people that opened up before him, the tears he'd refused to shed for all those years wet his cheeks as he took in the sight of his blood-soaked Mate. Completely back in human form, his footsteps faltered until Lore looked up at him and smiled.

"Get your ass up here, Dragon Man. It looks way worse than it is, and I'm in serious need of a hug."

Taking the last few steps and climbing up on the gurney in record time, he gently lifted his Tigress onto his lap. Carefully inspecting her back and finding it healed, he held her close to his chest and closed his arms around her.

"Thank you, mo ghrá. Thank you for everything," he whispered into her mind as he kissed the top of her head.

"Shouldn't I be thanking you? I seem to remember some big, bad Warrior saving my ass."

"But I was only strong enough to break the unfathomable hold Malvolia had over me because of you. It was your strength, your belief in me, and the inherent, unending love I have for you, my Fated Mate that allowed me to break decades...centuries of captivity."

"Whoa there, Sable. This whole Mate thing...I'm not...I don't..."

"You will," he chuckled. *"But we'll talk later. Right now, there's a room full of people waiting to talk to us."*

Smiling at the chaotic thoughts running through his Mate's fantastic mind, Sable found his brother in the crowd. Breathing a sigh of relief when Stone gave him a single nod, his smile grew when his twin spoke through their unique connection, telepathically apologizing, *"I am so fucking sorry. That bitch had us all locked down."*

Only able to nod and wink in response as Carrick, Head Elder of the Golden Fire Clan and one of the most prominent, respected and oldest Guardsman in existence appeared before him, Sable straightened his back and held his head high. He'd only seen the man a couple of times, and that had been when he was but a boy.

Waiting for words of recrimination for letting the Elder's Goddaughter come to harm, the Paladin was shocked speechless when Carrick held out his hand and proudly smiled "I could've picked no better a Mate for my dear Lorelei." Shaking Carrick's hand, Sable could only hold on tight as he absorbed the waves of ancient Dragon magic as the Elder added, "Thank you for your continued service to Dragon Kin. You are a credit to all of us, past, present, and future. Should you ever have need of me, you only need to call."

Taking a step back and turning to the side, the Elder held out his hand and continued, "May I introduce, Draco, Original Warrior, and Guardian of the Dragons."

"Holy shit," Lore gasped. *"That's Draco, like the real fucking Draco. The guy who called the Dragon to life. Damn..."*

"Uh-huh," was the only response Sable could come up with as he too was in complete and total shock.

Bright red hair with a full, thick beard to match, the Guardian wore a billowy white shirt and a kilt in the tartan of the First Dragon. A great mountain of a man, a true Highlander if ever there was one, stepped forward, bowed his head, and acknowledged in a brogue so thick Sable understood about half of what he said, "Yoo've made us prood, son, an' yer lass is a true Warriur froom an honored bloodline."

"I think he likes us," Lore's amazement sounded in his mind. *"Can you thank him for both of us, Dragon Man? My brain is sorta fried."*

With barely the time to do as his Mate requested before Carrick was preparing to introduce another of the newcomers, Sable felt incredibly overwhelmed and more than a little phobic with all the people staring at him. Decades spent alone or being tortured left him ill-prepared for everything going on around him. Had it not been for Lore in his lap, holding his hand and rubbing her thumb over the pulse in his wrist, he had no doubt he would've already been braving the frozen out of doors to escape all the unwanted and unneeded attention.

Keeping up with his duties as Head Elder in the room, Carrick led a tall, ethereal woman with hair the color of sunshine and translucent skin the serene, calming hue of a summer sky. "Sable, Lore, this is the First Elder, an Ancient One of the Highest Order, Shavon. She, along with King Alarick, have charge of the Council of Oracles." Turning the full dominance of his gaze onto Sable, he added, "It is she who is responsible for the *Rún Naofa* you carry within your soul."

Taking hold of her elegant hand as she held it out before him, Sable found it hard to remain upright when his fingers touched hers. The jolt of supremacy, the flash of eternity, and the depth of her unconditional love for all things living was nothing short of a revelation. One that was put into words when Lore breathed, "Wooooooow."

"Thank you, Queen Lorelei. That is an incredible compliment coming from someone of your grace and authority."

"And I thank you," Sable stepped in for his suddenly tongue-tied Mate, her shock at being called Queen a little more than she was prepared to handle. "For your trust in me all these many years."

Her smile quite literally brightened the room as she leaned forward, placed her forehead on their still-joined hands, and praised, "The honor is all mine. You have exceeded the expectations of every Oracle. You give us hope." Lifting her eyes, she looked first to Lore and then to him before adding, "Live well, for you are the future we have been praying for."

Head swimming, hardly able to fathom what her words truly meant, Sable held Lore tighter still as he telepathically whispered, *"I'll give you a million dollars to get me the hell outta here."*

"Not until I get to meet you," the young blond with eyes as blue as a summer sky and a smile that exuded nothing but pure joy giggled as she walked right past Carrick. "Sorry, I have a bad habit of eavesdropping." Holding out her hand, she pulled both he and Lore into a generous, loving hug before stepping back and introducing herself. "My name is Sydney; Sydney Kavanaugh and the title they've given me really doesn't matter. What *is* important is that I'm so delighted to finally meet you two. I've read a lot about you both."

Untangling herself from his arms and scooting to the very edge of his lap, Lore slowly shook her head as she marveled, "You're the Sydney from the Golden Fire Clan. The little girl born of two humans, both from the bloodline of the original Mage. You embody the spirit of the last full-blooded female Dragon born of a King and Queen, and you were taken to the Refuge." Everything she said, all of it speeding by so quickly that it took Sable a minute to catch up, was said as a statement, not a question.

Fearing his incredibly eager Mate had offended at least one, if not all of the dignitaries in the room, Sable opened his mouth to apologize, but he never got to utter a word as Lore went right on without missing a beat. "But weren't you only five or six when you left? And wasn't that like three-and-a-half or four years ago?"

Blushing and nodding, Sydney shyly confirmed, "Right you are! I heard you were a smart one, and you haven't let me down."

"Then how are you...umm...well..." At a loss for words, Lore ended up using her own makeshift hand signals to ask the young woman how she'd gone from a child of six to a full-grown woman of at least her mid to late twenties as she tried to distract with another question. "And why are you back? I thought you were to remain at the Citadel pretty much forever."

Chuckling with a cute little wrinkle of her nose that made her look even younger, Sydney replied, "Well, only Fate, Destiny, and the Universe truly know what's in the works for any of us, and in my case..." She fidgeted with a curl that framed her face. "Well, you're probably gonna laugh at me." She paused again for just a second then added with a chuckle, "But here goes...I've been called back to give my Mate a much-needed wake-up call."

Walking up behind her with a knowing smile on his face, Carrick laid his hand on her shoulder. "But no one knows she's here and as you can imagine; her return is going to take some explaining." Stopping to look at everyone in the room, he only began again when his gaze landed on Sable and Lore. "So, I have to swear everyone here to secrecy until Sydney has had time to reconnect with her parents."

A chorus of *yes, aye, and absolutely* filled the room right before Lore asked, "Sorry to be a pain in the ass..."

"But she always is, and she always will be. My bestie has to have answers to *all* her questions, or she'll drive you absolutely crazy until she figures it out," Minka teased from somewhere over Sable's shoulder. It was reassuring to know his Mate would always have her closest friend, come what may.

Looking up at Carrick then to Shavon, Sydney waited until she'd gotten a nod from both of them before she answered, "I completely understand. Shavon can tell you that I'm the same way. I need those answers. I have to understand. All I can tell you right now is that time works differently at the Citadel." Closing the distance to the side of the bed, she laid her hand on Lore's and winked before adding, "But you'll see for yourself soon enough."

CHAPTER FIFTEEN

*H*ours had passed. Conversations that should've been had were glossed over or put on hold until Sable felt better...even as she wondered if he ever would.

"Yes, yes he will," she adamantly declared to herself. "I'll make damned sure of it."

Stepping out of the best shower of her entire life, she took her time drying off, putting on her favorite lavender lotion and braiding her hair. Walking out into her room, Lore was sadder than she'd expected to see that Sable was gone. She could admit to herself, if no one else, that she liked being alone with him. Sure, he was a mess of shattered pieces - kind of like her very own Humpty Dumpty, but he was smart with a quick wit and had a way for understanding her sarcastic sense of humor that no other person she'd ever met possessed.

"And if my mother were here she would say, 'That's because he's your Mate, Lorelei. He was made just for you, and the Universe does not make mistakes.' Damn, if that woman didn't have all the answers."

Sitting on the edge of the bed and looking at the colossal

snow scene her Grandma had painted, she thought about the day she'd found Sable. Remembered being drawn to the exact spot where he was buried. Was it really true that Fate wouldn't be denied? Had it been the hand of the Universe or Destiny or some other deity that led her there? She'd probably never know.

So, where was he now?

With her hand on the doorknob, she took a deep breath, let it out as she counted to ten, plastered on a smile, and opened the door. Walking down the hall, the voices of the others growing louder with every step, she thought about turning around, thought about finding Sable, packing a bag, and hitting the snowy trail, but knew one or all of them would just come looking...and ultimately find them.

Crossing the threshold into the large, open great room, she gave a wave and cheerfully asked, "Anybody want any coffee?"

"Already making the second pot," Minka's cheerful response came from the kitchen.

Spinning on the balls of her stocking feet, Lore headed straight into the kitchen, put one hand on her hip and the other on her best friend's head then asked, "Are you feelin' okay? You don't have a fever."

"Yeah, sure. Why would I have a fever? Have you lost your mind...again?" The Snow Leopard snickered her reply, not looking up from the muffins and cookies she was putting out on a tray.

"Well, let me see..." Lore tapped the end of her chin with the tip of her index finger as she very purposely furrowed her brow. "You've never made a cup of coffee on your own that didn't come out of a pod, and even then, the machine is programmed to do everything but push the damned button. You eat dry cereal out of the box because, and I quote, "Getting a bowl outta the cupboard and the milk outta the fridge is a lotta work just to have breakfast. This way, I can keep it with me in case I need a snack before lunch." And, let us not forget, just last week when you cut the mold off of a piece of bread, slathered it in peanut butter and told me you'd be okay 'cause you weren't allergic to penicillin."

Still not looking up even as the muscle in her jaw clenched and unclenched from where she was trying to keep from smiling, Minka shrugged as she mumbled, "Maybe I like these guys."

Happy her friend had *finally* met people, other than herself, that she truly liked, Lore just couldn't let Minka off the hook without giving her a rash of shit. Slapping her hand to her chest and gasping aloud, she blurted out, "Say it ain't so. Oh, my Goddess, am I dreamin'? Could it really be happenin'? Whatever will I..."

"Shut up, Asshole."

"That's Miss Asshole to you."

"Soon, to be Mrs. Asshole," Minka snickered, finally looking up but only to bat her eyes and throw a loud smooch in Lore's direction.

"Low blow, Dork. How long have you been holdin' onto that one?"

"Since you carted that Dragon home on your back through a blizzard, cleaned him up, made sure he was comfortable and swore he wasn't dead even though he looked like a man-sized popsicle." Raising an eyebrow and leveling her gaze, the Leopard added, "He's been important to you from the first moment you knew he existed. At least, admit it to me since you can't admit it to yourself."

"I seriously hate you," Lore grumbled under her breath.

"No, you don't. You love me. You're just scared. And there's not a soul alive who would blame you."

"Ain't that the damned truth?" Annika chimed in as she entered the room. "Is this a private meeting, or can anyone join?" Continuing to talk although neither Lore or Minka had answered her, the Vixen chuckled, "Meeting Stone kicked me in the ass, threw me for a loop, and tied all nine of my tails into knots."

Rolling her eyes, still pissed at the way the Arctisune and her Mate had stormed into her Clinic and all but accused her of hurting Sable, Lore sarcastically sighed, "Yeah, come on in." Not acknowledging what Annika had said, Lore charged on, her anger renewing with little to no effort. "Since you're already here, you can tell me what the *fuck* you were thinkin'? A little explanation, maybe? An I'm sorry for busting in the joint and letting your asshole of a Mate try to put a sword through my ass?"

Looking truly sorry, her usually bright silver eyes turning the deep gray of a snowy sky, Annika leaned her butt against the counter on the opposite side of the kitchen and shoved her hands in the pockets of her jeans. "Ya' know, I don't have a good explanation or even a bad one. Hell, I can't even come up with an excuse that doesn't sound like horseshit except, I'm a dumbass? I should've called no matter what Stone said." Exhaling sharply, her eyes still meeting Lore's she went on, "He could hear Sable. Feel his pain, his confusion, the utter hopelessness inside of him, and freaked the hell out. He kept saying that Sable was giving up, that he was gonna die so that no one got that damned 'Secret' thing. Like a silly girl in love, I wanted to make it all better."

"When we left home, I had no clue where we were going. The trail Stone saw in his mind went all the way out past the gorge, cut through the valley, and went up the steep side of the big mountain."

"'Cause that's the way I brought Sable here after I found him frozen solid with no heartbeat buried in the snow."

"Once I saw where we were, I could've...I should've...Oh hell, I fucked up, Lore, and I'm sorry." Pushing away from the counter, she stopped after two steps and pulled her hands from her pockets, holding them out, silently asking for a hug. "Can you forgive me?"

"It's not her you need to forgive." Stone's deep voice rolled into the room. "It's me. She would've had to knock me out and tie me up to keep me from busting in here like SEAL Team 7." Stopping when he got to Annika's side, he nodded, "So, be mad at me. Hell, hate me forever, but not Nika. She loves you like a sister and would end up hating me if you couldn't forgive her."

Staring at Stone, she could feel the honesty of his words, his sincere regret at the way he'd acted, and a shit ton of hope that she would find it in her heart to forgive not only Annika but also him. Biting the inside of her lip, she looked at Minka, who gave her a single nod then turned back to the Arctisune and her Dragon.

"Yeah, all right. You're forgiven, but you're paying to fix every damn thing you broke and volunteering every Saturday for the next six months at the Clinic helping me give shots to the large predators."

"That's the best deal I've heard all day." Holding out his hand, Stone waited patiently until Lore finally took it. Smiling as he shook her hand, confirming their agreement, he whooped, "Dammit all, you're absolutely perfect for my brother."

"Speaking of Sable, where did he go?"

"I thought he was with you." A look of concern dropped over his face as he let go of her hand and turned towards the door. "I haven't seen him since you guys went to shower and change."

Right behind Stone, sure Sable had just needed a few minutes by himself, she spoke her thoughts aloud as she went back over the last conversation she and Sable had had. "He took his shower first. We sat there in silence, content to hold hands until I couldn't stand how bad I itched from the dried blood all over me. I got up to shower. When I got out, he was gone. I figured he was out here. I got distracted when I heard Minka in the kitchen and the rest..." She shrugged, feeling utterly useless for not knowing where her Dragon was. "Well, you know the rest."

Stepping up beside Stone before dashing in front of him and taking the lead, Lore remembered the bond she shared with Sable. Opening the doors and locks as she split her consciousness between where she was and her direct link to the Paladin, she used her best joking tone as she called out, *"Tired of me already?"*

Tuning out the echo of Stone, Annika, and Minka's boot heels on the metal stairs, she tried again, *"Where ya' hidin'? Minka's made coffee and she actually opened a box of cookies and defrosted some muffins. Remember how I told you she can't boil water? Well, she can open boxes. Come on. You've got to be hungry."*

Moving faster and faster the more time that ticked by in which she got no response, Lore deactivated the locks on the last door with little more than a thought, something she tried to never do, and pushed it open with such force, the crash of the metal handle against the block wall echoed through the empty lab. "Fan out," she ordered. "He's got to be here."

Throwing her senses as wide as they would go, she searched every exam room then to be sure she'd hadn't missed him, opened every door and turned on every light. By the time she reached the very last room, in the farthest corridor, on the side of the Clinic they hadn't even used yet, her heart was in her throat, and sweat was pouring down her back. Reaching for the light switch at the same time that she opened the door, and audible sigh of relief flew across her lips as her eyes landed on Sable's back.

"Hey, Dragon Man. Whatcha doin' down here?" She asked, referring not only to how far from everyone else he'd gone, but also why he was sitting on a cold, steel examination table, shoulders hunched forward while he stared at an empty, unpainted wall. "Didn't ya' hear me callin'?" The sound of his steady breathing filling the silence, she feared the worst while hoping against all hope she was wrong when he still didn't answer. Unable to wait a second longer, she crossed the room, and with the cheeriest voice she could get together in less than a second after being scared shitless, tried to effuse calming support. "Sable? Hun? You okay?"

"No...No, I don't think I am...or that I'll ever be."

Slipping right into doctor...or veterinarian mode, as the case may be, Lore felt his head, looked at the whites of his eyes, and listened to the strong, steady beat of his heart. "What doesn't feel right? What hurts? What ..."

Shaking his head, still looking at his clasped hands as they hung limply between his legs, Sable sighed heavily, "Everything. Nothing. I'm a fucking waste of space, broken, worthless, trapped in my own head, running from enemies who don't exist."

Snapping his head towards her, the action stiff and robotic - entirely unlike the man she was getting to know, Lore saw the elliptical pupils of his Dragon a split-second before his voice dropped at least an octave and the next words he spoke were laced with a thick Scottish brogue, not unlike Jewel's. "If ye caur fur heem at aw, yoo'll git th' Ancient, th' Guardian, an' th' Princess. Me lad's tried tae lock awa' th' demons af his past insteid af dealin' wi' them, an' th' bastards ur 'bout ta break free."

Trying *not* to act shocked, like she talked to millennia-old Dragon Kings every day all day, Lore made some goofy gesture that any other time she would've been embarrassed by just to keep from pointing at him like he was Elvis at the Bellagio, as she confirmed, "You're Sable's Dragon, right?"

"Is 'at important noo?" He acerbically growled before

going right on ahead and answering her question with a metric ton of irritation coloring his tone, "Yes, Ah am. Noo, help yer Mate, coz af Ah hae tae, he'll nae be back by yer side fur quite a loong time...if e'er."

"What do you mean? I thought you could cure damn near anything in the Paladin you were joined with."

"Ah kin, but in Sable's case, Ah'll need th' help af me Brethren, an' they're nae af this earth."

Gone as quickly as he'd appeared, leaving her hanging with a revelation that absolutely blew her mind, Lore schooled her features just as Sable's eyes turned back to a beautiful hazel, and he continued right where he'd left off like nothing had happened, "I can't shake the feeling that it was too easy to kill Malvolia." Turning on the bed and grabbing her hands, he leaned forward, almost begging her to believe what he was saying, "Do you know how many times I tried to strike out at her, tried to get the upper hand, tried to get away, tried to kill her? Hell, tried to kill all the other mother-fuckers so that Dragon Kin... the whole fucking world would be okay?"

The rage in his voice, the shake of his hands, the appearance of the granite scales of his Dragon superimposing over his skin all spelled trouble. She had to get him to Shavon and the others or them to him before something that couldn't be fixed blew up in her face.

"Don't you think I want to get this fucking Secret, or Truth, or whatever the fuck it is outta my soul? But what good would that do? I would be dooming someone else to a living hell. At least, I'm used to it." The harsh, sarcastic laugh that followed his snarled words was almost as worrisome as the way his hands were rapidly heating up against hers.

Not letting go no matter how hot his skin got, Lore stood up and nodded, "I can't begin to fathom what you've been through. Calling it hell on earth is like saying the Grand

Canyon's an ant hill. But you know that it's gonna take time. You're gonna need to give yourself a fucking break. Let yourself heal. You can't make up for centuries of captivity in the blink of an eye."

Pulling him to his feet and inching back towards the door, she kept talking, praying she was distracting him enough to get him upstairs. "Give the damned Runny No Fo, or whatever it's called to me. I'll carry it for a while. You said it was as easy as shoving it into my soul. So, do it. Isn't that what being a Mate is all about? Putting the other person first?" When he didn't respond only looked at her like she'd spoken in another language or had three heads, she added, "Dammit, I'm not good with all the mushy stuff. I'm saying that I think I'm falling in love with you, and I want to...*have to* help in any way I can."

CHAPTER SIXTEEN

$\mathcal{W}$ith every step he took the staticky murmurs in his mind grew louder. It brought back memories of the shortwave radio the guards used to listen to or more aptly, run the dial from one end to the other again and *again*. The damned thing never got a clear signal, but the sons of bitches refused to give up and admit defeat. If they could make out the words, or at the very least a tune, they left the damn thing playing for days and days on end.

Bits and pieces of conversations and a word here or there jumbled up with a buzzing so much like an angry swarm of bees that the hair on the back of his neck stood on end was all he could hear. No matter how loud, nothing remotely coherent developed. Nothing like the ghosts of the past or the demonic hauntings threatening his sanity, these voices had a message...something he consciously knew he absolutely *needed* to hear.

Tuning out everything and everyone around him, he concentrated on only the noise between his ears. There had to be a way to bring out the conversation, to leave the static behind and figure out what he was missing.

"You okay, Sab?" Stone asked, his tone heavy with concern as his hand landed on his shoulder and squeezed the knotted muscle.

Shrugging off his twin's touch, he pointed at his ear as he shook his head, knowing his twin would understand and not take offense at being made to wait. There was no backing down or turning away, even Herne was tuned in and listening. Together, they would get to the bottom of the new signals or...go a little crazier trying.

Letting himself be led through the heavy steel door at the top of the steps then down the hall, more words became audible as tiny bits of the static receded. Now, all he needed to do was figure out what language they were speaking. The dialect had a sing-songy syncopation with sporadic guttural sounds he thought were being used as inflection.

"Do you know what they're saying?" He asked Herne, hoping the ancient Dragon King could at least head him in the right direction.

"Ah've got nae feckin' idea an' Ah thooght Ah'd heard it all."

Not waiting until they were in the great room, he pulled his hand from Lore's and headed straight for Shavon. Shocked when Lore appeared at his side and returned her hand to his then holding tight, he worked *not* to be irritated with her suddenly smothering attention.

"I'm okay. I would tell you if I wasn't. Just need to speak with Shavon for a minute, if you don't mind," he projected directly into her mind.

"Okay."

Her tone sounded hurt, or maybe it was resentful, he really couldn't tell and cursed his social ineptitude and awkwardness from years in captivity. Not ever wanting to cause his Mate any pain, he immediately squeezed her hand and softened his tone as he reassured, *"But you are more than welcome to come along."*

Relieved when the Ancient One ended her conversation with Carrick and turned towards him at the same time as Sydney, he smiled politely when Shavon beamed invitingly. "I like that you kept your beard."

"Me too," Sydney quickly agreed, adding, "It makes you look wild and mysterious."

Unable to hold back a chuckle, he teased, "Wild, maybe. Mysterious, not even close. I kinda feel like everyone who sees me is thinking, 'there goes the crazy Dragon. Wonder what they did to him? How did he survive? Will he ever be normal?' And I left the beard because I really have no clue how to shave with anything but a straight razor. The Overlords loved to feed me tidbits of the outside world. It was one of the ways they'd torture me. Goddess knows they were always looking for new inventive ways to make my life miserable, to make me give up what they thought I knew. Let me have magazines, newspapers, listen to the radio. Later on, it was video games and the internet. Then they'd snatch them away and leave me completely alone, in the dark, with nothing for months and months."

"I am so sorry. Wish I could raise them from the dead just to kill them all over again," Lore immediately offered. Clearing her throat and throwing a new emotion as if it were a different hat, her over attentiveness grated on his nerves as she added, "I can get you a new razor. Maybe an electric one, so you don't cut yourself."

"Well, I think you should keep the beard," Shavon chimed in, giving him the slightest of winks. "And the long hair. Only change it if you want to. Find out what you like. Find a way to be comfortable in your own skin. No one expects you to snap your fingers and begin anew like the past centuries didn't happen."

Waggling her eyebrows, Sydney teased, "And with your

tattoos, all you need is a leather jacket and a Harley. You'd be Hell's Angels chic."

"Indeed," Shavon clapped with delight. "I believe your brother has quite a few motorbikes."

"Motor*cycles*," Sydney corrected, adding with a giggle, "You've got to excuse Shavon, she doesn't have much time for pop culture."

Laughing along with all three ladies, Sable waited until there was a lull in the fun before stepping a bit closer to Shavon. "I think I need your help."

Glancing at one another then back to him, Shavon and Sydney spoke in unison, "Absolutely. Anything you need."

Glancing at Lore, who was suddenly disinterested and looking at Carrick and Draco as they stood to the side debating the politics of revealing Dragon Kin to the humans, his eyes returned to the Ancient One and the Princess as he explained, "I hear the weirdest sounds." Tapping his temple, he hurried to clarify. "Not voices like all the other times. Nothing I've ever heard before. It's weird. No. It's ...well... it's..." Letting out a sharp exhale, he stopped trying to explain and cut to the chase, "Can you just listen for yourselves and tell me what fresh hell is trying to boil over up there?"

"Of course, we can," Shavon replied. "But I'm sure it's nothing as bad as you're imagining."

"After everything you've survived, it's natural for you to think the worst. Never fear, Shavon can figure anything out," Sydney finished with a bright, reassuring smile.

"Thank you, both." It occurred to him that he might have sounded a little too desperate or overly eager, but he was both and there was really no reason to hide either from two people as powerful as the ladies before him. If he knew anything, it was that they were aware of so much more than any other and had probably seen him coming a mile away.

Hardly feeling their gentle slide into his mind, Sable

waited patiently as the ladies literally divided his mind between them with each taking half. While Shavon's magic felt like the soft glow of candlelight, Sydney's was as bright and happy as the sun. Both were a welcome change from the dark, cold chaos he usually experienced.

With his eyes bouncing from one woman's face to the other, he looked for any indication that they'd figured it out. Grinning when Shavon spoke directly to Herne in Gaelic, Sable promised himself to remember how formal and respectful the Dragon King had been to the Ancient one so he could tease the old boy when they were alone. It wasn't but a moment later that he felt both women backing out of his mind.

Keeping his eyes on Shavon, his heart jumped into his throat when she shook her head, "I found nothing."

"Me neither," Sydney shrugged.

"So, you've never heard that language before? Don't know the translation?"

Leaning forward, Shavon laid her hand on his arm. Silver sparkles swirled in her eyes as the scent of the ocean filled his senses along with a deep sense of calming reassurance. "No, Sable, we didn't hear anything."

"What?!" Louder than he'd expected with the sharp tone of disbelief, he furiously shook his head as he growled, "You can't hear anything?"

"Nope," Sydney repeated, adding, "Not even the murmur of your memories. It's silent except for your Dragon King."

"And he confirmed what you said and allowed me to listen to his memories. But as far as hearing them for ourselves..." Shavon removed her hand from his arm and stepped back to stand beside Sydney. "There's nothing there to hear."

"This makes no sense," he protested. "They're right here." He jerked his hand from Lore's and beat the heels of his hands against his temples. "They're trying to tell me something. Wait..." He stopped hitting himself and held his breath, but there was nothing. Cupping his hands over his ears, he slammed metaphysical plugs in both his ears and still there was nothing.

Staring at Shavon, he could only murmur, "They're... just...gone."

"They're what?" The Ancient One's brows furrowed as the silver of her eyes turned a dark blue and deep purple.

"Gone. Silent. No longer there."

"Maybe you just need to get some rest," Stone suggested, coming up on Sable's left side. "To sleep and heal. Let Herne take over for a while. Let your mind recuperate. You've got to be mentally, physically, *hell, everything* exhausted."

Stepping closer, her arm brushing him, Lore was suddenly very attentive, the entirety of her focus on him as she patted their clasped hands with her free one. "Stone's right. You need to get all rested up." Giving him a wink, her smile grew exponentially, she beamed, "Because I am ready to be Mrs. Lorelai Lauder like yesterday."

Shocked into silence, looking down at his Mate as if seeing her for the first time, he couldn't help but wonder what had happened to make her change her mind so drastically in the last few hours. Snapping his eyes to Minka's, feeling the Leopard's serious concern from all the way across the huge room full of people, he instantly opened a unique mental link to her as she spat, *"What the fuck? Did you slip my girl a mickey?"*

"What's a mickey?"

"Oh crap, I forgot, you probably aren't up on popular slang. I'll explain later." Minka rolled her eyes as she went on, *"Suffice it to say, either Lore's been drugged, or she's lost her mind. One minute she's doing everything she can to convince herself and anybody who calls her on it that y'all aren't meant to be together, aren't Fated Mates and*

all that happy horseshit then in the blink of an eye, she basically asks you to marry her?"

"She also offered to carry the Rún Naofa when she found me in the Clinic."

"She did what?!" Minka's screech echoed through his mind.

"So, that's not normal?" He hated that he had to ask what was and wasn't strange for his Mate, but he knew Minka would be honest...probably brutally so and wasn't disappointed by her response.

"Not even close." Minka was getting louder with every syllable, her frustration, and confusion sparking from her mind to his.

"I wondered. I mean, I have no clue about women. The only one I've been around in the last century or so was a stark raving lunatic of a Witch who wanted to rip out my entrails and use them to decorate her hovel in Hell."

"Ouch!" Minka sucked her teeth. *"That's some gruesome imagery there, Dragon."*

Unable to answer as Lore cleared her throat and tugged on his arm, Sable was once again flabbergasted as she got down on one knee and with the sweetest of smiles, almost too sweet for the strong, self-possessed, intelligent woman he knew her to be, proposed, "Will you, Sable Lauder, be my Mate forever and always?"

Thankful when the room erupted in a chorus of congratulations and whoops and hollers, Sable forced a smile at the same time that Minka exclaimed, *"Son of a bitch, she's caught your crazy, Dragon Man, and I'm gonna kick it right outta her ass. Unless you beat me to it."*

CHAPTER SEVENTEEN

*W*hat the hell just came out of her mouth? Why had she said that? Better yet, what the hell was she gonna do to get out of it? Had someone slipped catnip into her water? She knew for a fact she hadn't gotten into the tequila. Hell, she hadn't even had a damn cup of coffee.

If it was 1958 and she was in the movie *Brain Eaters*, she'd swear one of the creepy alien wormy things had crawled into her brain and was running the show. But it wasn't, and she wasn't, and no spaceships had landed on the island, so she had no clue what was happening.

The one and only bright spot? Sable looked as shell shocked as she felt. Maybe they were having a shared psychotic episode. How fucked up had her life become that she was praying she and the Dragon she'd dug out of the snow were sharing a psychosis? Maybe if she laughed really loud and yelled, "Candid Camera," everyone would laugh along, and she could forget the insanity of the last ninety seconds.

No such luck...

"A toast to my brother and his Mate," Stone cheered as he held his beer high over his head. "May they know the love and happiness I've found with Annika. Nobody deserves it more than my big brother."

"Get your ass up off that floor," Minka's snarl slashed through her mind.

Looking down at the hardwood floor, or more to the point her knee on said floor, Lore spat right back, *"What the fuck is going on, Min? If this is one of your stupid practical jokes, I swear to the Goddess, I'll shave you bald and throw your ass out in the snow in your bra and panties."*

"No, no, no, no," her bestie adamantly, and really loudly, denied. *"This was all you, Sour Puss. I had nothin' to do with it."*

On her feet and plastering on a smile, Lore switched 'channels,' as she thought of the different unique pathways that allowed her to privately telepathically speak to others, from Minka to Sable. *"Ummm, I'm gonna sound like a real dick, but..."*

"Let me guess, you really don't want to be my Mate. It was supposed to be a joke, but now you're stuck and want me to help get you outta it." It was a statement, not a question, and delivered with so much intensity and vehemence that Lore felt it was necessary to defend herself.

"Hold on there, tall, dark, and scaly, I didn't say any of that." Righteously pissed off and letting her anger get the best of her, she charged on, *"What I was going to say was that I definitely did not plan to do this in front of everyone. That we need to get to know each other before making plans for Mating Ceremonies and happily-fucking-ever-after. How about we have a real fucking conversation. Stop the madness for one gods-be-damned second and find out exactly why the Universe made us for each other and Fate is so all-fired ready to throw us together. Wouldn't you like to know the woman you'll be stuck with for the rest of forever and then some?"*

Holding up her index finger when he started to answer

her rhetorical question, she shook her head and grabbed his hand. Ignoring everyone's stares right along with the instantaneous silence that fell over the whole crowd like a ton of bricks, she dragged him out of the room.

Moving as quickly as she could with a whole shit ton of pissed off Dragon in tow, she made a quick right, hot-footed it down the hall, and ducked into her den. Flipping on the light as she jerked Sable through the door then kicked it closed, she spun back towards him and let out a sharp exhale.

Dropping his hand, she ran her fingers through her hair, her go-to move when she was thinking or frustrated or both and attempted to explain. "Look, I don't know if it's all the crap that's been going on, the having huge chunks of skin ripped off my back and healing it up in record time, or all the people in my house when some days having Minka here is too much for me, but something is seriously fucking with my mind."

Needing to work off some of the nervous energy zapping through her body so she could reason out what had made her get down on one knee like Princess Charming and propose to Sable, Lore began to furiously pace while her Tigress prowled the confines of her mind. "First of all, and let me make this perfectly clear, I will admit right here and now that I *know* you are Mate." Beating the tips of the fingers on her left hand against her chest, she kept right on going. "Yes, I fought it. Yes, I denied it. And both were done out of fear. I hate to say it. It pisses me off, but it's the truth. I was scared *shitless*. And, while I'm doing my version of true confessions, I'm pretty sure I'm falling in love with you."

"Yeah, you said that before."

Ignoring Sable's gruff sarcasm, she kept right on going, "Just like you, I've heard all the stories about Fate not being denied and how if we fight what's meant to be all kinds of terrible shit will happen to us and those we love until we finally give in to what the Universe wants."

"Nothing new there. I've never had a choice. Why should I have one, now?"

Continuing to ignore his snarky cynicism, no matter how disconcerting it was, she went on, "But I absolutely refuse to make a commitment like an official Mating blessed by your Elders, the Universe, the Goddess, and whoever else has to bless it, until I know we are both ready." Retrieving a scrunchy from her front pocket, she wound her hair into a messy bun as she kept on explaining. "I might as well admit that I've never really had a boyfriend. Sure, I've been on dates, been to parties, had one too many shots and made out with some rando whose name I didn't know and never wanted to know."

The low growl emanating from somewhere deep in Sable's chest shouldn't have made her feel good...*hell, almost giddy*, but it did. Just another thing she had to be pissed off about.

"But an honest-to-goodness, let's-carve-our-names-in-a-tree, I'll-wear-your-class-ring, you're-my-boyfriend-I'm-you're-girlfriend kinda relationship - I've never had. Never found anyone I liked well enough to make that kind of commitment." Turning on her toes and heading back the way she'd just come, she went on, "Hold on. There's more. Here comes the big reveal and if you laugh, I swear I'll kick you right in the balls, I'm still a virgin, and I swore to myself I'd stay that way until I found my one and only."

Strategically letting that last tidbit fall when she was all the way across the room, Lore also stopped pacing and finally looked up. Meeting Sable's stare head-on, she added, "So, I hope you can see why I have to be sure. I have to know..."

"You have to know that the batshit crazy Dragon won't lose whatever marbles he has left, run off to parts unknown, and break your heart?"

Was he being obtuse, just an asshole, or a little bit of both? Sure, he was saying the right words, but his tone, not to mention the rigid set of his shoulders, the manic clenching and unclenching of his fists, and the furious flames dancing in his eyes said he was nowhere near on the same page that she was. Suddenly flustered, not understanding what she'd said to piss him off, Lore took a step forward.

Searching for the words to make him understand, to make him see that she was laying all her cards on the table, she took a deep breath, and that's when it hit her - something had changed. Not just a little bit, but earth-shattering, complete one-eighty, not-on-the-same-planet changed.

His scent was off. His aura had gone from the pale rainbow colors of a man in a stage of healing and rebirth with the want and need for a future to a murky brown with horrible gray overtones of an angry, destructive man who wanted to hurt and maim that made a shiver slither down her spine.

"I don't think you would ever intentionally break my heart."

"But you do think I would fuck up and that I'm batshit crazy?"

There it was, a rasp, almost a lisp or a hiss just under his harsh snarl. It was familiar, eerily so, but Lore simply couldn't place it. She had to keep him talking. Needed to get him to give up at least a hint at what was going on. What had changed? Why he was so angry...so hateful.

Opening her mouth to speak, she instead found herself falling backward. Arms flailing and air flying from her lungs as an invisible fist punched her in the gut, the last thing she heard before her head bounced off the red brick hearth of the fireplace and she lost consciousness was Sable roaring, "Stop! No! I won't let you!"

CHAPTER EIGHTEEN

*W*ith no idea where he was or how he'd gotten there, the only thing that mattered to Sable was saving his Mate from the grotesque, faceless, hooded monstrosity trying to consume her in one gaping-maw bite. Launching himself over the back of the enormous brown leather sectional bisecting the room, he slid across the glass top coffee table on his hip and grabbed her ankle with an iron grip.

The second his skin touched hers a flash of unholy mysticism shot up his arm and attacked his heart before sucking both he and Lore into a swirling spinning portal so full of evil taint and horrific black magic that it scorched his clothing and singed his hair. Literally climbing her body while struggling to pull her closer, the instant her body was flush with his, he wound his much larger frame around her, preparing for what he was certain would be a painful landing.

Even more so than he'd expected, his shoulders hit the concrete with a bone-jarring thud. The crack of bones and the all-too-familiar tearing of tendons filled his ears before he forced himself to roll ass-over-teakettle into what felt like a brick wall. Pain was something he was used to and easy for him to ignore, but his fear that Lore had been hurt beat at his heart and soul like a jackhammer ripping through concrete.

Throwing open his preternatural senses as far and wide as they would go, he surveilled the area for anything or anyone malevolent. First and foremost, he must protect his Mate. Too much had already happened. She'd suffered far too greatly because of him. Was it any wonder she wanted nothing to do with being tied to him for the rest of her life?

"I don't even want to be with me any longer than I have to," he scoffed under his breath. "Time heals all wounds. Isn't that a saying?" Huffing a sarcastic laugh, he added, "Not only am I talking to myself, but I'm also asking and answering my own questions. Time to find a padded cell far from this frozen rock."

Sure he was alone with Lore, the Paladin ever-so-carefully stretched his legs and loosened his arms from around her back. Slowly maneuvering until he was sitting upright with his back against the wall he'd just crashed into, he shifted Lore on his lap, cradling her head in the crook of his arm. Healing magic tickled his flesh as the wound on her head was knit back together courtesy of the Tigress with whom she shared her soul.

Seething that she'd once again been hurt on his watch, he spat, "I just can't see a way where this will ever work. Someone is always going to be after me, trying to rip the Secret from my soul. How will I keep her safe?"

"*Yoo will dae whit ye hae tae dae, Laddie. Noow, stop yer belly-achin'. Control whit ye can control. Fix whit ye can fix. Donnae go wishin' fur mair feckin' trooble.*"

"Thanks for the pep talk, Herne. You're so motivational," he sighed aloud while taking a second to look around.

Instantly shocked at where he was, his eyes zeroed in on an unusually large, exceptionally dark, incredibly still crimson stain in the center of the floor. Images flashed in his mind. The demons of the past reared their ugly heads. Taunts and slurs he'd hoped to never again experience rang in his ears.

Back in the mausoleum. Back to where he'd escaped to save Stone. Back where they'd taken his tongue. Back where he'd prayed for death.

"But why here? Why now?"

"Because sometimes shit just happens."

Unaware he'd been speaking aloud until he heard the sound of Lore's groggy voice, Sable couldn't help but smile as he looked down at her beautiful face. Petite features, such elegance in the arch of her eyebrows, the Cupid's bow of her upper lip, the way her long, dark lashes perfectly rimmed her eyes - all of it was a beautifully deceptive mask for the fierce predator that lay beneath. One he admired more than he had the words to express.

Pulling himself away from the musings of a fool, he was forced to admit, if only to himself, that she was not only gorgeous but so very right. Sometimes shit did just happen. Whether it was Fate or Destiny or just a cosmic collision that no one foresaw, there were only ever two choices - forge ahead or give up and giving up had never been, nor would it ever be, an option for him.

Whatever he'd done to be blessed with a Mate like her made all the shit that just kept happening so very worthwhile. Unfortunately, the look she gave him said she was having more than second thoughts about her recent proposal, and more to the point - *him*...

Before he could utter a word, Lore sat up, rolled off his lap and onto her knees, and as gracefully as he imagined her Tigress moved, crawled nearly ten feet away. Clocking her every move, he held his breath as she carefully placed her butt on the concrete then gently leaned back against the base of an entire wall of sarcophagi doors.

Knowing they had only minutes before the next pile of crap came cascading towards them and unable to stand the emotional and physical distance between them, Sable tried his hand at sarcasm by chuckling, "Already having cold feet?"

Snapping her eyes to his, their dark brown depths filled to the brim with anger and frustration was terrible enough, but it was the heartache he saw weaving in and around everything else that felt like a dagger to his soul. Topped with the fact that it was all aimed at him was more painful than all the torture he'd ever endured.

Biting his tongue, he forced himself to wait for her to speak. Long seconds turned into agonizing minutes while Lore continued to glare at him. Watching as the wheels of her mind turned over and over, he couldn't help but wonder what he could do to undo whatever pain he'd caused.

Narrowing her eyes and letting out an exasperated sigh, her gaze dropped to her hands and tartly asked, "Are you trying to be funny, or are you really just an asshole?"

"I was going for funny but from the tone of your voice, I'm guessin' I missed the mark."

"You damned sure did," she shot back. "I poured my heart out to you. Told you things no one, and I mean *no one*, but Minka knows about me. Really personal things. And you mocked me, made me feel like an idiot then..."

"I did what?!" Immediately incensed. Sick and tired of being everyone's whipping boy, something inside him snapped. There was no more holding back. No more keeping his mouth shut. If she wanted to see the real him, then he'd give it to her, but not before he let her know that she was not blameless in whatever was going on between them. "I made *you* feel like an idiot? How the hell do you think I felt when you got down on one knee and proposed to me? DO you have any idea?" Not waiting for an answer, the words bubbling out of him like water from a broken dam, he railed on, "Like a fucking moron! A big fucking butt of the joke. That's how. Right there in front of the Ancient One, the Original Warrior, Carrick, my brother. What the fuck were you thinking? Was it a game? A joke you and your friend cooked up to make me look even stupider, less worthy than I already am?"

Mirroring his movements, Lore leaped to her feet and flew across the room. Jabbing him in the chest with the tip of her index finger, she spat, "I wasn't, 'cause that wasn't me, Dumbass. You had to know that. Any fucking idiot could see...'"

"Could see what? How would I have known that? Or anything? I don't know you at all."

"Exactly! But I fucking know you."

So much pain, so much vehemence, so much rage was in every stab of her finger. Yes, she was yelling at him, but so much more was at play. Regrettably, he had his own issues making everything a million times worse as he continued to listen.

"You're a Dick. A heartless, callous, unfeeling jerk who only wants what he wants when he wants it with no regard for others or what they're feeling. You are supposed..."

Grabbing her finger before she struck him again, Sable pulled her flush against his body and wrapped his arms around her. Looking right into her eyes, he ground out through gritted teeth, "Stop. Stop right now. Something is very wrong. *Very wrong*. This isn't..."

Doing everything in her power to pound her fists against his chest, he thanked the Goddess that he'd penned her hands between their bodies, but that didn't stop her from snarling, "It damned sure is. I was wrong to *ever* think I could ever love you."

Intellectually, he knew she was pissed and not thinking about what she was saying. She'd been hurt and wanted to strike back. Emotionally, her words hurt worse than any whip ever had. For one fleeting moment, he'd had hope. With every word that flew from her mouth, that hope was being extinguished.

Sure, he'd survived worse, and the thought of giving up, of walking away held a certain appeal. It was a choice he'd never had before, but that was the coward's way out, and Sable Lauder was no fucking coward. Confused? Yes. Unsure how to navigate the treacherous waters of any relationship, especially one that involved his heart? Hell yeah! But there was no way he was giving up the one good thing in his life without one hell of a fight.

Squeezing her closer, just enough to shock her into silence, he quickly spoke directly into her mind, *"Stop fighting me and listen."*

Shocked when she did as he said, he hurried on, *"Thank you. Now, let me see your memories from when you came to get me in the Clinic until you say I mocked you."*

"You did. You..."

"Alright. I did. Whatever you say. Just open your mind, and let me see...please."

The fight within her was so strong. A real credit to her character, to the type of leader she would be when the time came... to the kind of Mate he would need her to be if he was ever to live whatever passed for a normal life.

Part of her wanted to give in and do as he'd asked while her incredibly independent spirit refused to back down without a fight. Refused to be the first one to surrender.

Seeing how much it would cost her to go along with his request, Sable relented, *"Okay, you look at mine."*

Not waiting for an answer, he pushed his memories through their Mating bond. Watching as the anger literally melted from her expression, he took his first easy breath when she cursed, *"What the hell? Have the Body Snatchers come to Baffin Island?"*

CHAPTER NINETEEN

"*I gotta see this shit again,*" she muttered, not waiting for Sable to respond. More shocking than the first time, it damned sure looked like her. But there was no way in hell it was her. Was there? Talk about a total mindfuck. *Freaky Friday* had nothing on the shit she was seeing in Sable's mind.

"*This is just too fucking freaky,*" she huffed. "*Now, it's your turn.*" Pushing her memories of the worst moments in her life, Lore immediately wished for the ability to take back what she'd just said when Sable's shoulders slumped and true, palpable regret filled every fiber of his being.

Trying to stop the recollection, pull it back from his mind, at the very least stop it and erase what he'd seen, she grabbed his upper arms and shook until his eyes reluctantly met hers. Suffocating in his guilt, remorse, and self-recrimination, Lore did the only thing she could think of - pushed up on her toes, wrapped her hand around his neck, pulled his face to hers, and kissed him as hard and quick as she could.

Forcing him to open, letting everything she felt for him, all the feelings she'd been trying to deny, hide, shove to the side, and run away from flow freely, she inhaled his gasp when he blessedly returned her kiss. Lost in a wondrous sea of emotions she'd never thought she was capable of feeling was nothing short of miraculous, but it was having those soul-deep sentiments reciprocated by the only man who'd ever touched her heart that had her climbing his body.

Loving the feel of his hands on her ass and the way he held her tight to his chest, Lore instinctually wrapped her legs around his waist. Any other time, the feel of his hard, thick erection against her center would've had her ending their kiss and making excuses to get away as quickly as possible, but with Sable, she never wanted it to end.

Trying to find the words to tell him how very sorry she was for losing her temper and spewing such hateful vitriol, she trailed kisses along his jaw as she breathed, "So...so sorr..."

Clap! Clap! Clap!

Feeling as if she'd just been doused with a fire hose of frigid water as the mocking echo of a slow insulting clap echoed through the mausoleum. Driving she and her Dragon apart, Lore unwound her legs and pushed off Sable's huge body, spinning towards the obnoxious sound before her feet hit the ground. Side-by-side with her Mate, she slid her eyes to the side, happy to find him just as ready for battle as she.

Never one to wait, eyes trained on the same hooded Ghoul she'd seen in Sable's memories, the Tigress snarled, "Show yourself, Asshole. 'Nuff with the games!"

Stopping just inside the ornate stone archway, the Phantom floated mere inches above the ground, its tattered robes billowed in the blustery wind it brought along for the ride as its raspy reply filled the air with evil taint as it slithered towards them. "Young love. What a sssssssshame neither of you will live long enough to enjoy it."

Counting down from five, the number of seconds her father said separated the scoundrels from the honorable, Lore envisioned ripping the head from the Ghoul and grinding its bones to dust. She'd seen Sable's memories. Knew the fucking piece of shit had brought her Mate back to this very place to taunt him...to break him. It was the bastard's last-ditch effort to finally shatter not only the man's but the Dragon King's spirit. Filth, plain and simple. Willing to do whatever, no matter how vile to get what it wanted.

"Not on my watch, you worthless piece of shit," she grumbled under her breath. "Never on my watch."

No sooner had the words crossed her lips than two skeletal fingers appeared from under the threadbare cuff of the bastard's robe and with nothing more than a flick, Lore was airborne.

Flung backward as if she was lighter than a feather, the air was forced from her lungs, and her brain rattled in her skull when her back slammed against the farthest rock wall. Impaled by one of the large iron handles of a sarcophagus door, she could only take shallow gasps or risk puncturing a lung with the jagged edges of her broken ribs, but that didn't stop her mind.

"*LORE!*" Sable roared, fear and fury thick in his tone.

"*I-I'm o-okay,*" she panted. "*Don-Don't you dare t-take y-your eyes off that motherfucker. Kill it d-dead.*"

Eyes glued to the back of her Mate; Lore sought a calm she didn't feel. Manifesting it out of sheer determination, she held on tight and let it flow directly to Sable. She needed him to find his focus. She needed him to fight. She needed him to kick ass and take fucking names. For too long he'd done nothing but survive. It was time for him to live, and if it took every last breath in her body, she would help him do it.

But damn it all to hell, reaching him was proving harder than she'd ever imagined. Frozen where she'd left him, a vengeful rage, fiery fury, and burning wrath flooded his mind and body consuming all his thoughts.

No time to unravel the chaos and calm him down. Time for plan B. No molly-coddling and cheerleading for her Dragon. He needed a kick in the proverbial ass, and she was just the one to give it to him. All she had to do was find a way to drown out the venom the ghoul was spewing.

"Give me the SSSSSSecret. Releasssssse it to me."

"Never!" Sable ground out through gritted teeth. "Kill me, and you'll never get it."

Running the tips of its skeletal fingers around Sable's neck, across his shoulder, and down his back, the soulless black nothingness that served as the Ghoul's eyes looked right at Lore as he hissed, "Oh, dear SSSSSSable. There are sssssssso many thingssssssss worsssssssse than death."

Snapping its fingers, a cat 'o nine tails appeared out of thin air. Hovering just behind her Dragon, the nine barbed lashes swung backward and forward, long, hooked spikes getting closer to his back with every sway.

Hurrying to shift through the incoherence and madness the mere thought of torture conjured in Sable's mind, Lore stumbled on an image that brought her to a screeching halt. Tucked away, covered in layer after layer of pure-white, powerful Dragon magic, her dear, dear Mate held tight to a memory of none other than her.

There she was, fast asleep, head on his bed in the Clinic, her hand holding his. She hadn't even known he was awake at the time. Had no idea he'd been aware she was there. But he had, and it seemed that he was using that image as an anchor to keep himself from being consumed by the hate and rage threatening his very sanity.

"What a fool I've been," she sighed. "Hope I live long enough to kick my own ass and beg for his forgiveness."

With no time to dwell on past mistakes, no time to tell Sable that everything would be okay, and unable to move the smallest muscle, Lore let her eyes slide closed. Metaphysically reaching for the bones of her ancestors, feeling their power igniting in her veins the closer she got to their final resting place, she beckoned the ancient Inuit mysticism that was her birthright.

Using her soul as a conduit and her mind the navigator, she filled the bond she shared with her Dragon with the cool crisp splendor of the enchantment of the indigenous people of the Arctic. Sensing the solidity and stability, the perfect combination of two ancient Warrior Clans, she added the warm fierce mysticism of her Tigress.

Absorbing the ripples of power fueling Sable and his Dragon King, she spoke the words Shaman Lorelai Ashevak, her very own grandmother had spoken on the day of Lore's first transformation, "Accept the power of the Tigress. Embrace the strength of Her soul. Hold fast in the belief that you are worthy. Today is the first day of your New Beginning."

Inhaling as deeply as she could, not worrying about broken ribs or punctured lungs, she heaved every ounce of magic, power, strength, belief, and most importantly love that she had straight into her Dragon. Hitting his soul at the precise second nine razor-sharp barbs slashed through his shirt and ripped into the skin of his back, Lore watched the perfect coalescence of Dragon and Tigress in the heart and soul of her Mate.

Throwing back his head, Sable's roar shook the rafters of the centuries-old mausoleum. Breaking free of the ghoul's taint, her Dragon reached over his shoulder, and in one fluid motion tore the spikes from his back, swung them over his head, and heaved them towards the ghoul.

Caught in the propeller-like motion of the cat 'o nine tails, the specter stumbled backward, shrieking with fury as the lashes tied it tight to a seven-foot wrought iron candelabra. Watching with tears of pride filling her eyes as Sable reached no less than ten-feet tall with the white-striped fur of her Tigress sliding down his back and covering his arms, she telepathically cheered him on. It was the most spectacular sight she'd ever seen as he flashed across the room, wrapped his massive paw around the bastard's neck, and ripped the hood from its head, cursing, "No more games, Bitch. Today you die!"

CHAPTER TWENTY

*W*ith her body snapping forward and backward like a rubber band, the magic holding her hostage was suddenly and painfully severed. Smacking the ground with a bone-jarring thud, her ass felt like it was almost on her shoulders before she had time to figure out what fresh hell had befallen them. Up on her feet, ignoring the searing pain beating on every damn nerve she had, Lore's blurry vision cleared just enough for her to see Sable holding a mummified Malvolia high in the air by the neck.

Fighting to stay on her feet as she gave her best impression of charging forward, Lore made it halfway to her Mate when a realization almost too fanciful to consider popped up right in front of her. Holding her hands up, she had to blink twice and shake her head to believe what she saw – no fur, no skin, only sparkling gray scales from the tips of her fingers all the way to her shoulders.

Looking down, she found the same covering the rest of her body. Armor, an *impenetrable scaled defense*, exactly like Sable had worn when he battled the evil Witch in Lore's Clinic. But how? Were she and her Mate starring in the paranormal version of *17 Again*? George Burns was a classic, but *this* was just too much.

Before reaching any plausible, or implausible for that matter, conclusion, her thoughts were cut off by Malvolia's unholy shriek. Begging for mercy, sobbing and wailing, pleading with lies that she'd been the only reason Sable had survived the vicious Overlords, the Witch's voice became more of a wheeze as the Paladin squeezed ever harder.

"No more, Witch. No more will you prey on the innocent, torture the unwilling, and take what is not yours. Today will be the end of you," Sable snarled. Squeezing tighter, the long talons of the Tigress inhabiting his soul ripped through the paper-thin skin of Malvolia's neck. Black goo shot from each puncture, decorating the walls and floor with a grotesque mosaic of death and destruction, but the Paladin continued his torture.

Scratching at his fur, opening and closing her mouth, gasping for air like a fish out of water, Malvolia wheezed, "If... If I d-die...sssssssso do you."

"Then, so be it!" He boomed, the snap and crack of the brittle bones of her neck filled the mausoleum.

"NO!" Lore roared, unwittingly shooting Dragon fire from her mouth as she yelled.

Pushing a gawking Sable out of the way, she pounced on Malvolia in hopes of putting out the blaze. Straddling the Sorceress, she smothered the flames with her scale-covered hands, scattering the still-glowing embers.

Planting her palms on the stone floor on either side of the Witch's head, Lore shoved her shortened snout against Malvolia's crooked nose and spat, "Explain yourself, or I'll take my chances and kill you myself."

Still panting, trying to catch her breath as the wrinkled, translucent skin of her neck slowly knit itself back together, the bitch continued to act smug, almost superior, as she rasped, "Do you think I'm daft, little girl? Of coursssssssse, I tied his life forccccccce to ..." Cut off by a hacking cough followed by more fetid, black sludge dripping from her mouth, Malvolia's lips actually curved into a vicious sneer as she hissed, "Mine. Insssssssurance, Sssssssweety."

Moving so quickly Lore hadn't seen it coming, Sable lifted the Witch off the ground and in one fluid motion sent her smashing into the far wall. Then, before Malvolia had time to catch her breath, he snatched her once again by the neck and as he beat her back against the wall, roared, "Then to hell with both of us."

Fear and fury clashed in a monumental explosion that sent Lore flying across the room towards her Dragon. She would not lose her Mate. She would not let him kill himself in the name of whatever mantle of self-hatred and self-sacrifice he held onto. Sable would live if it was the last thing she did.

Not willing to chance using the Dragon fire again, especially since she had no idea how to control it and with only five strides left until she was upon Sable and Malvolia, Lore did the only thing left to do, scream for help, *"Dragon King? Time to wake up and join the fight!"*

"Bin haur th' whole feckin' time. Did ye hink ye called th' fire on yer oown, Lass? Nae e'en yoo're 'at guid." His roar rattled the confines of her mind at the exact same second a broadsword appeared in her right hand and a bowie knife in her left. Cocky didn't begin to describe the ancient Dragon, which at any other time would have disgusted her to no end, but in this case, he was more than earning the right. Turning control of her body over to him before he asked, she let out the breath she'd been holding and said a prayer to any Diety who had the time to listen.

"Lae thes tae me," the Dragon King added, the thrill of battle heavy in his tone as he rammed both blades straight through the Witch's torso.

"Noooooooo!" Roared Sable a split-second before Lore's hand swung out to the side and tapped him in the chest.

Watching her Mate crumble to the ground, she screamed both telepathically and aloud, "What the fuck did you do?"

"Poot uir laddie tae sleep fur a bit. We need tae deal wit thes witch an' he's jist in th' way."

"Yeah, okay, but I'm rolling over on you like a school bus in traffic when he wakes up ready to kick somebody's ass."

"Aye, see 'at ye dae, Lassie," Herne responded as he swung her body back towards the Witch.

Still hanging on the wall like a piece of gruesome folk art, Malvolia's feet peddled at the air while she struggled to remove the blades. Black, rancid gunk flowed freely from her new wounds, sizzling and steaming as it puddled on the stone floor.

Watching her own scale-covered hands slam the Witch's shoulders to the wall was freaky enough, but when Herne's deep, Scottish rumble came from her lips, Lore wondered if she was in the weirdest ever episode of the *Twilight Zone*. Holding fast to her belief that this was the only way to save Sable and rid the world of one of the evilest Witches she'd ever encountered, Lore embraced the primal Dragon magic flowing through her veins, effortlessly letting her own Inuit and Tigress enchantment join the mix.

"Let's see whit yoo've concocted, Witch," Herne sneered. "Oor are ye a liar as weel as Satan's Consort?"

Ebony sludge splashed on the pewter scales covering Lore's face as Malvolia screeched, "You'll find nothing, Dragon Bastard." Spitting again, the acidic slurry popping like water in hot oil against her scales, she jeered, "I'll feed your bones to the Hounds. Eat your entrails for my supper. Drink your blood from the Dark Lord's chalice. I might've run from that blue-skinned freak, but I'll never fear the likes of you."

Ignoring her spits and curses, the Dragon King's fiery magic slashed through her body just as his sword and knife had her skin and bone. Ripping through her mind, tearing through her sorcery, and shredding the shriveling rotted core of what used to be her soul, he was merciless in his mission. Refusing to give up, he delved deeper, fought harder and just when Lore was losing hope, he zeroed in on a small glowing ember no bigger than a dime tucked away in the deepest recesses of Malvolia's psyche.

With no fear or trepidation, Herne's mysticism stalked towards what Lore immediately recognized as a Madstone. Unable to fathom how Malvolia had turned what her ancestors used as powerful medicine into something so absolutely evil; Lore was shocked when Herne answered her question before it was asked.

"Malvolia's nearly as auld as time. She's bastardized and tainted everythin' she's ever tooched, but she'll nae git uir Laddie, no as loong as Ah live."

Loving the grumpy old cuss a little more every second she spent in his presence, Lore held her breath as a huge metaphysical Dragon paw reached out and grabbed the sanguine Madstone. Appearing in her hand in the space between her snout and the Sorceress' face, both Dragon King and Lore glared into Malvolia's soulless eyes.

"Soo, thes is hoo yoo've stayed alive aw these years. Sucked th' life frae mah laddie. Drenched yer polluted Madstone in his bluid an' magic." Giving her an extra shake, one that quite literally rattled the rotted teeth in her mouth, he snapped, "Ah'll pray fur th' sools fa foond nae escape..."

Said as a statement and not a question with an intense hatred that made Lore's own being quake, Herne leaned her head forward until it pushed against the tip of Malvolia's nose. Holding the Madstone just enough to the side so the

Witch could witness what he was doing, the Dragon King snarled through gritted teeth. "It ends haur."

Screaming and begging, Malvolia's words quickly devolved into garbled gurgles of indistinguishable goobledy-gook that both Herne and Lore happily ignored. Closing Lore's fist as tight as he could, the Dragon King ground the Madstone into a fine powder before opening his hand and letting the billowy wind take it away.

"Watch noo, Lass. Watch thes bitch fade tae doost an' disappear oan th' win' ne'er tae return. Knoo 'at yoo've saved our Lad."

Receding to the back of her mind, his final words echoed through her mind. *"Yoo'll doo fine, Lore. Jist fine by oir Sable. Ah cooldn't hae picked better meself."*

CHAPTER TWENTY-ONE

Sitting straight up at the same time his eyes snapped open, Sable glanced at the spot where he'd last seen the Witch. Up on his feet and straight to the wall, all he found was a puddle of the nasty black tar that served as Malvolia's blood and two holes where blades had been forced into the stone.

"Where could she be?" He thought aloud. "If Herne..."

"Dead."

The single word answer, spoken with no emotion felt like the confirmation he'd been longing to hear, but the ensuing silence had him spinning around wondering if yet another foe had risen from the depths of Hell. Locking eyes with Lore, every muscle in his body froze.

Wearing the armor of his Warrior Dragon, she looked like a gorgeous Avenging Angel. Although not any taller or broader, her commanding air filled the room. She was the stuff of legends. He thought of all the great female Dragons and the stories of their prowess in battle. Not a one had anything on his Mate.

Then it dawned on him, if she was wearing the scales of his Dragon...

Even before his hands were up to his face, Lore confirmed, "Oh yeah, you're still wearing my fur." Holding up her own hand and twisting front-to-back and back-to-front, she added, "And if it's all the same to you, I'd like it back."

"How did this happen?" He blurted out, not exactly ignoring her question but so shocked all semblance of manners flew out the window.

Rolling her eyes to look at the ceiling as she let out a long-suffering sigh, Lore dropped her chin to her chest and admitted in a completely irritated tone, "I'm pretty sure I did it."

"What was that again?" He asked, adding a chuckle to let her know he in no way blamed her and actually found the whole thing rather comical.

Raising her head, Lore threw back her shoulders and held her head high as she began to explain. Just another sign of her fortitude and forthrightness. Lore was goodness and integrity personified, and he would thank the Universe every day of his life for her.

"This entire place..." She pointed at the sarcophagi, the alter, the beautifully stitched tapestries. "Is full of my ancestors. Well, my *ananaksaq's*..."

"Your grandmother's family," he interjected, chest swelling with pride when she looked surprised that he knew Inuit.

"Yes," she winked and nodded. "Good job, Dragon Man. I'm impressed. Not many take the time to learn a language so unique." Giving him a second wink, she went right on, "Anyway, when I was hanging like a ragdoll on that wall over there..." She gave a sideways nod of her head. "The only thing I could think to do was gather up all their magic and throw it to you. I thought it would help you take down the Witch." Biting the inside of her cheek and looking everywhere but at him, her voice got softer as she admitted, "And... I grabbed too much."

Taking a deep breath, she finally looked back to his eyes as she rushed on, talking so fast it took him a minute to catch up. "I just didn't want anything to happen to you. You know, this thing between us freaks me the hell out but I just *know* we need to give it a try. Like a *real* try. We need to see if it works. I know I'm falling in love with you, dammit, and it feels right. Hell, I might even already be in love with you. Then there was that whole thing back at the house."

Throwing her hands out in front of her chest and shaking them as if she could erase the memories, she kept right on going. "I know that wasn't you, but it still hurt like hell. But now I have to wonder if I should've told you anything at all. Maybe you think I'm a freak or there's something wrong with me. I promise it's not that. It's just that I was raised to believe that there are things that are sacred, most of all our bodies. They are the gift we were given by the Heavens', the Universe, our families. And, I made a promise to *my* family, our Shaman who was my grandma, to the Great Mother, and especially to myself to wait until I found my Mate. The one man in the entire world meant to be mine. Does that..."

Moving across the room in the span of a heartbeat, Sable wrapped Lore up in his arms and held her tight. Looking into her one blue and one brown eye with the elongated pupils of his Dragon staring back at him, Sable spoke straight from his heart. "Even though it wasn't truly me being a supreme jack-ass, I'm still so very sorry I hurt you."

"Oh, I know. Really, I do. I just..."

Laying his furry index finger on her lips, he smiled when she huffed and narrowed her eyes but refused to be deterred. Continuing on, it was his turn to reveal something to her. "I need you to know that you are not the only one in uncharted territory when it comes to love of any kind. When I said the *only woman* I'd been near in centuries was Malvolia, I wasn't exaggerating."

Leaning down, he placed a chaste kiss on her lips, praying she understood that it was not only an affirmation that what he was telling her was the truth, but most of all, it was a promise. Lifting his head, he smiled at the love he saw shining in her eyes and whispered, "From this moment forward, we do everything together, including making love for the very first time. Deal?"

"Ah..." Forced to clear her throat to continue, Lore sheepishly grinned as she sharply exhaled before nodding, "Absolutely." With her grin turning into a sassy smile, she added, "As long as you get me outta these scales and back into my fur."

"You got it," he readily agreed then giving her a wink to add his own cheekiness to the conversation added, "'Cause I've got a score to settle with a certain Dragon King and his high-handed way of knocking me on my ass."

"Yeah, I told him you were gonna be pissed. But I have to admit he kicked some serious butt."

Loosening his hold on his Mate, Sable waited until she stood beside him before walking them to a set of chairs in the farthest corner. Listening as she talked, he took a seat and pulled her onto his lap.

Stopping mid-sentence, Lore's eyes popped to his as she asked, "Is this necessary? There's a seat right there, and I'm sure even with the armor I'll fit."

"Yes, it is *very* necessary," was the only answer he gave her. His independent, strong-willed Tigress would have to understand that he may not be like other Dragons in a lot of ways, but when it came to needing her right beside him at all times, Sable was all Alpha Dragon, all the time and she was his Mate.

Waiting patiently as she scooched and scooted to get

comfortable before continuing with her retelling of what had happened, Sable was finally forced to lay his hand on her arm and admit, "If you keep rubbing you're luscious behind across my lap, I won't be responsible for what happens next."

Whipping her head to the side, her eyes as big as saucers and her mouth in the shape of a perfect 'O,' Lore whispered, "Noted."

Without moving another muscle, she explained in explicit detail everything that occurred after Herne put the whammy on Sable. More than once, he cringed at the danger Lore had been in and cursed his Dragon King's highhanded ways, but just as he was able to call Herne to the forefront of Lore's mind, his Mate laid her hand upon his cheek and with an honesty that rang so clear and so true Sable's anger simply melted away, she reassured, "King Herne is truly one of a kind. He loves you like a son, like his very own. Every single thing he did today was for you. To atone for all the centuries he was held captive, unable to protect you from the years of torture and pain."

Wrinkling her nose, cute even though it was covered with tiny pewter scales and a bit wider than usual, she added, "There is no doubt that what he did was cavalier and incredibly inconsiderate, the King pushes his title as far as he possibly can, but it was all done out of love. Never forget that."

Unable to hold back any longer, Sable slammed his lips to Lore's. Immediately demanding entrance, his heart soared when she didn't hesitate to open completely to him. They were finally on even footing. Right where they were supposed to be. Where he'd longed to be for so very, *very* long.

Then a loud, "Ahem" drove them apart.

On his feet and shoving Lore behind him in the same graceful motion, Sable's roar was cut short when his eyes fell on Shavon and Sydney. Adding to his embarrassment was the knowing grin on both their faces that all his stuttered and stammered apologies only made grow wider.

Lifting her hand from under her long, sky-blue, woolen coat, her silver eyes shining brightly, Shavon gently shook her head, "No need to apologize. We are only here to set things right." Motioning between them, she added, "Swap fur for scales as it were, and get you both back home."

Before he could speak, Lore popped out from behind him and with a jaunty whoop, cheered as she bumped his thigh with her hip and waggled the tiny 'eyebrows' above her gorgeous Dragoness eyes, "Thank the Goddess. I've got nothin' against my man's scales, hell what woman wouldn't like to be dressed in sparkles? But, I gotta admit, he wears them way better than I do."

CHAPTER TWENTY-TWO

"*S*o, she faked her death because seeing Shavon freaked her out?" Minka shook her head before turning towards Shavon and lifting her hand for a high five. "Girl, you're a serious badass. I love it. Always said women make better Warriors than any dude ever could."

Lore chuckled at her bestie's 80's way of talking. It was one of the many, *many* things she truly loved about the crazy Snow Leopard.

"You know it," Sydney jumped up from her place on the bed and slapped Minka's hand when Shavon didn't. "It's one of the things I'm kinda dreading about going home. The whole 'I am Dragon Guard hear me roar' stuff I know my dad and all my uncles are gonna throw at me. The title of 'fragile flower' doesn't exactly fit."

Turning in her seat in front of the mirror, Lore batted at the air and shook her head, "You have nothing to worry about, Syd. You exude strength and poise." Pausing for a second to be sure the young woman *knew* that the Tigress saw the *real* her, she nodded and smiled, "Sure, seeing as you're full grown is gonna be one helluva shock. I can't imagine the adjustment your parents will need to make. 'Specially your dad, if he's anything like mine was. I was his little Princess even when I transformed into a huge Siberian Tigress."

"No joke," Minka readily agreed. "Lore's dad was so damned smart and dignified, but just let my girl here try to break out on her own, do something he hadn't been allowed to think about for a damned month of Sundays, and the old man would literally try to ground her."

"And I was nowhere near still a teenager."

"Oh, no, he didn't?" Sydney laughed. "How old were you?"

"Fifty-two in human years."

"No way!" Sydney gasped with a huge grin on her face and a twinkle in her eye. "I can see my dad trying to do that, too."

"He's gonna be so damned happy to see you nothing else is gonna matter," Annika chimed in for her place on the bed. "You know better than most that all those Dragons have soft underbellies with even softer, mushier hearts," she added with a chuckle that had everyone else giggling and nodding.

"Just stand your ground. Make him see you for who you are not, not the little girl he knew. Sure, your situation is different than mine. You went on a serious growth spurt." She snorted with laughter. "But I have no doubt he loves you more than gummy bears and M&M's. It may take him a minute to adjust, but he'll fall in line. Look at me, I fought the whole 'Mate thing,' and here I am getting mated to a man I dug out of the snow less than a month ago."

"I'm sure you're right."

Glad she could help the young woman, even if it was in her own backass, messed up way, Lore turned back to the mirror to finish what little makeup she could stand putting on. Butterflies were throwing a rave in her tummy, and her Tigress was pacing the confines of her mind. Today was the day she'd dreamt of since she was a little girl, but honestly never thought would come.

In less than an hour, she would be mated to the man the Universe made just for her. It was a dream come true. The road to get where they were had been full of potholes, but she and Sable had done it...*together*.

Even though Stone was a wise-crackin' son-of-gun that loved to tease her until she wanted to wring his neck, Lore would always be thankful that he'd made time to reconnect with her Dragon. It had indeed been something both men needed whether they wanted to admit it or not. The final piece missing from their incredibly special, one-of-a-kind connection Malvolia and her Overlords had forced Sable to sever all those many years ago.

"Time will heal all wounds." Grandma Lorelai's voice echoed through her mind. Damn it all if that old lady wasn't always right. The brothers still had roads to travel and wounds to heal, but now they had the time to do it and Lore couldn't be happier.

Looking up, she caught a conspiratorial glance pass between Shavon and Sydney right before the Ancient One got to her feet. Stepping forward, she laid her hand on Lore's shoulder and smiled, "I must go check on the preparations. Everything needs to be perfect."

Laying her hand over Shavon's, Lore met the Ancient One's gaze in the mirror. "Thank you so very much for everything."

"It is my pleasure, Dear. You and Sable deserve nothing but happiness and joy." Patting Lore's shoulder once again, she added, "But off I go. I'd hate to have Jewel come looking for me. That Nymph runs a tight ship."

Gone as soon as she'd uttered the last word, the only proof Shavon had been there was the fragrant scent of sand and sea and the melodic ringing of her laughter that she left in her wake. Sliding her eyes to Sydney, Lore held no pretense as she almost demanded but with a smile on her face, "Spill,

Chick-a-Dee. What was that look between you and tall, beautiful, and blue?"

"And don't try denying it," Minka jumped right in. "I saw it, too."

With a shy giggle, Sydney shrugged before proposing a deal, "Get into your gown, and I'll tell you everything."

"But," Lore rebutted. "I have to finish my hair and makeup."

Playfully swatting her on the shoulder, Minka teased, "You're already gorgeous. Get your ass up and let's get you dressed. I'm dying to know what's going on."

"Is it *your* Mating day?"

"Hell, no! But as the Leopard of Honor, a title I've given myself mind you, I'm obliged to give you a hard time."

"Yeah, yeah, yeah," Lore snickered with a sigh, deciding it was easier to do as her best friend wanted than try to put on makeup she didn't care about.

Getting up, she turned towards the bed to find Sydney holding the dress her mother had worn on the day she'd mated her father. Soft woolen, as white as the new-fallen snow, the fabric had been woven by her mother. Everything within their Pride and Tribe was a family affair, but weddings topped the cake.

The breathtaking off-the-shoulder A-line gown had been designed by her dad's mom and sewn by her Grandma Lorelei. Absolutely nothing was left to chance, and every single detail had meaning and significance.

White to signify not only the frozen land that they called home but the pelt of the majestic animal with whom she shared her soul and the purity of the love a Tigress feels for her one true fated Mate. Black fur decorated the swoop-neck décolletage and cuffs that gently wrapped around her wrists denoting the stripes of the Tigress and the rebirth of each Mate joining as one heart, one soul, one mind.

Perfectly formed crystals that Lore's father had dug from the Sacred Caves atop Mount Thor, a place of communion and unity for all Inuit Tribes, both Shifter and human. After midnight, the morning before the official ceremony, Lore's mother had sewn glittering silver thread in a vertical pattern running from neckline to hem that sparkled and shimmered like icicles hanging from the mountainside as the dress caught the light.

"I'd forgotten how beautiful it was," she breathed. "Pictures *did not* do it justice."

"It is stunning," Sydney readily agreed.

"Sure, is," Minka chimed in. "I admit, when you said it was wool I thought 'What the hell?' but this is awesome, Lore."

Taking off her robe, Lore stepped into the gown while Sydney held one side and Minka held the other. Sliding her arms into the sleeves, she felt as if her mother was with her, watching, guiding, making sure everything went exactly the way it was intended.

"Thanks, Mom," she silently prayed. *"I know you've always been here. Give dad and Ananaksaq a hug and kiss for me."*

Holding her breath as Minka lifted the zipper, Lore eyes never left Sydney's. Waiting for a response, a wail that she looked like Little Orphan Annie, laughter that she looked like a little girl playing dress-up, or *anything* that said she didn't look like a total doofus, Lore let out the breath she'd been holding when the younger woman gave a sharp, awestruck exhale before breathing, "Oh my Goddess, you are absolutely breathtaking. Sable won't be able to keep his eyes off of you."

"Or his hands," Minka teased, waggling her eyebrows and adding a wolf-whistle that had everyone laughing.

Spinning where she stood, it took a second for the image she saw in the mirror to register. No longer in a snowsuit, or a parka, or sweats, or Heavens forbid, a blood-covered set of scrubs, Lore looked like what her mom would've called 'a proper lady' for one of the only times in her life.

"Wow," was all she could say as the door swung open and Jewel came bustling in.

Instantly in tears, the Nymph flew across the room, wrapping Lore in a neck-breaking hug while her feet were still moving. "Oh, mah lassie, ye are mair bonnie than any bride Ah've ever seen." Pulling back while keeping her hands on the Tigress' upper arms, she hiccupped and sniffled as tears flowed freely down her cheeks. "Thank ye fur understandin' why Ah hid whoo Ah was froom ye. Mah heart woold ne'er heal if Ah thooght Ah'd lostt yer loove an' troost." Leaning in once again, she kissed Lore's cheek, adding, "Ah loove ye joost as much as Ah loove those two scoundrels and as Ah did their da and ma."

"Trust me, now that I know Sable, I understand completely why you did what you did." Giving Jewel another quick hug, she kissed the Nymph on the cheek and added, "Can't say I wouldn't have done the same thing."

Dropping her hands and stepping back, Jewel's head snapped towards Sydney. "When ur we..."

Frantically shaking her head, the younger woman shushed, "No. Not yet."

Sliding her eyes back to Lore, Jewel winked, "Och, jist wait, mah lass. Th' best is yit tae come."

CHAPTER TWENTY-THREE

*D*ressed in a surcoat just like he'd seen his father and the other Guardsman and Paladin of his Clan wear when he was but a child, recreated by the magic of the Ancient One, Sable stood watching the snow fall out the floor-to-ceiling windows that covered one entire side of the massive great room in Lore's home. It was hard to believe the day had finally come. The day he would stand before Creed, Carrick, Draco, and Shavon, before the Universe and every Ancestor and Ancient, with his brother at his side, to pledge his undying love and devotion to the one woman in all the world who calmed the demons of the past and made him feel whole.

Lore was nothing short of his very own miracle. She'd given him hope, shown him *how* to love, made him believe he could be respected and trusted and made him believe that absolutely nothing was impossible. Over his years with the Overlords and Malvolia, the Paladin never imagined he could have his very own happily ever after. It had been the fantasy that had kept him going. Always out of reach, but never far from his mind. And here it was. All he had to do was take the last few steps.

Walking up beside him, Stone bumped Sable's arm with his elbow and chuckled, "Got cold feet? Thinking about backing out?"

"Never."

"Well, then, you're gonna need this." Handing Sable a small pewter velvet pouch, he went on, "I was given specific orders from *Seanmhair* Sheena..."

"Dad's mom?"

"One and the same." Bumping shoulders, he chuckled, "Surprised you remember."

"I remember everything, Brother, absolutely everything. Those memories are all that kept me alive."

"And I am forever indebted to the Heavens and the Universe that they did," Stone nodded with a solemn look. "I never gave up, Sab. Never. I knew..."

"I know, Stone. *I* shut you out. I couldn't bear the thought of having you or your Dragon or *anyone* having to share that shit."

"Yeah," Stone looked down at his feet, his voice cracking just the tiniest bit. "I figured that was what you'd done. I wish you hadn't, but I understand why you did. Would've done the same thing myself."

"I also..."

"Need to tell me that you were tricked and went with the Overlords of your own free will?"

Astonished, Sable stammered, "H-How d-di you know?"

"I didn't. Not right away." His twin shook his head. "For the longest time, I couldn't figure out why you told me to turn back. Why you told me everything would be okay." Finally, looking up, he sniffed and rubbed his nose before smiling. "Then when I was in that fucking camp, heard your voice, felt your presence, it all made sense." Scratching at the scruff on his jaw, he added, "You always protected my ass from everything."

"You're my little brother."

Throwing back his head and laughing with a huge guffaw that sounded exactly like their father, Stone resounded, "By two damned minutes." He quickly turned, wrapping his twin in a tight hug. "Thank you for everything, Bro. I mean it. Everything damn thing. I love ya', ya' know?"

"Yeah, yeah, I do. Love ya' right back, ya' big lug."

Letting go as his brother stepped back, Sable watched a myriad of emotions rush across his twin's face before Stone donned his trademark cheeky grin and gave a quick lift of his chin. Once again holding out his hand, he teased, "Take this. You're gonna need it."

"Indeed you are," Shavon's lyrical voice drifted into the room right before the First Elder herself appeared at his side. "Open it up. Let us see what wonders lie in such a dainty package."

Carefully untying the silk ribbon, Sable held the corner between his thumb and forefinger before tipping the pouch towards the open palm of his other hand. Hardly able to believe his eyes when a perfectly round, sparkling diamond set in an intricately detailed platinum setting appeared. Nearly the size of the pad of his pinky finger, he instantly remembered seeing the ring on his grandmother's finger.

"Elegantly simple and absolutely beautiful," Shavon murmured.

"Just like Lore," Sable added.

"You are so right, Brother," Stone wholeheartedly agreed.

Lost in thought, his nerves finally catching up with him, Sable looked at his brother then to the Ancient One. Both were sporting wide, knowing smiles and nearly vibrating with excitement. "Alright," he scoffed. "What have you two got up your sleeves?"

Holding out her hands, Shavon waited until he had taken one and Stone the other before beaming, "I might have been keeping a secret."

"Oh?" Sable tried to act happy, but in all honesty, surprises were just not his thing. Never had been.

Nodding, her smile growing even more radiant, she continued, "Your official Mating ceremony will not be held here."

Feeling the growing presence of incredibly ancient, infinitely powerful magic, Sable narrowed his eyes and slowly shook his head. "You can't mean?"

"Oh, yes, my dear Sable," Shavon cheered. "You and your Tigress shall be mated in the Citadel."

Swept up in a swirling cloud of mysticism, all Sable could do was ride out the waves and wait for the second or two it would take before his feet touched the hallowed ground of the most sacred of all places. Although created and maintained by Dragonkin, the Citadel was revered by all those fortunate enough to be blessed by the Universe with extraordinary powers.

"Step out onto the lawn," Shavon's voice whispered into his mind before he walked in tandem with Stone, smiling at the way their 'twinness' had picked back up almost where they'd left off.

Shading his eyes from the brilliant sun with his hand to his forehead like a lazy salute, it was hard to fathom that the unextraordinary stone building before him housed some of the greatest minds, most supreme powers, and beings damn near as old as time itself. Holding out his hand for Shavon, he had to ask, "Where's Lore?" Hurrying to cover his anxious anticipation, he grinned, "I know you wouldn't kidnap me on my mating day and not bring her along."

"Absolutely not," the First Elder chuckled. "We just have

one little bit of business to handle, and you'll be on your way."

"Business?" Stone asked, eyes narrowing. "What's goin' on?"

Looking up at Sable then to his twin, Shavon slowly nodded, "Your brother has asked, and I have agreed, that he should no longer be the Bearer of the *Rún Naofa*. His priority and focus should be on Lore, their relationship, and any little ones who may happen along." Raising her eyebrows and scrunching her nose, she chuckled lightly, "I have a feeling the world is due a few more sets of Lauder twins."

"That's all on Sab," Stone quickly refuted, pointing and shaking his head as if he'd just been told he was about to be neutered. "Kids are not my thing. I'll make a damned fine uncle, though."

Looking at his brother through new eyes, for the first time, Sable saw fear. His loud-mouthed, rush-into-the-fight, kiss-ass twin was worried he'd fail as a father. Knowing nothing could be farther from the truth, he stowed the information away, promising himself to have a heart-to-heart with Stone later...when they were alone.

"No one knows what the future holds," Shavon mystically replied before turning back to Sable. "I just want to ask one more time, are you sure? I know your duty as the Bearer has cost you more than any other. I also know that you have been the most courageous, loyal, and steadfast. However, once it is removed, it immediately passes onto the next Bearer and your knowledge of this place..." She waved her hand towards the Citadel and the stunning countryside around it. "And the Oracles will be no more and no less than any other of your kind."

"Understood," Sable nodded. "Like I said when we talked before, I know being without the Secret will be different, I have no doubt I will miss the feeling of being a part of something so much bigger than myself. But I can't ask Lore to risk everything, to be my Mate, to put her life in danger, to protect the One Truth every day of our forever. It's…"

"It would've been nice if you'd asked Lore."

Spinning so quickly he almost lost his balance; Sable's eyes were captured by his gorgeous Mate's. More beautiful than anything he'd ever seen, dressed in a white gown that fit her like a glove with black fur and shimmering stones, Lore looked every bit the Queen she was meant to be…right down to her furrowed brow.

Stepping forward, Sable hurried to explain, "But I…Well, I just…"

Lifting the hem of her dress, his fiery Mate stomped across the courtyard, stopped right in front of him, and began poking him in the chest just as she'd done when they first met. "You just thought you'd make the very first big decision of our *entire lives* by yourself. Does that sum it up?"

"Well, …ummmmm. Yes, I guess it does."

Taking a step backward and lowering her chin, Lore took a deep breath before blowing it right back out. "Do you want to give it up? Do you want to stop being the Bearer? Or are you doing it because you have some half-assed, alpha-male-ego-trip going on that's telling you to 'take care of the little missus'?"

Trying hard not to laugh at his Mate's use of air quotes after she'd given Minka a ration of shit for doing the same thing, Sable did the only thing he knew would end their tiff and get them back on the road to happily ever after…he popped the question.

CHAPTER TWENTY-FOUR

Stunned silent for one of the only times she could remember in all her years, Lore worked hard to keep her mouth from dropping open in utter shock and awe when Sable got down on one knee, looking up at her as if she was his world. Her heart skipped a beat, and her hands started to shake as the love she saw in his eyes freely flowed from his soul to hers, filled the air around them and wrapped her up in a dream come true.

Gently holding her left hand in his right, he produced the most gorgeous and biggest diamond ring she'd ever seen. Sliding it barely onto her ring finger, he breathed the words Lore had honestly thought she would go to the Heavens without ever hearing from her one true fated Mate.

"Will you, Lorelei Bransfield be the love of my life, the beat of my heart, and my reason for being for all of eternity and then some?"

Opening her mouth and slamming it shut, wanting to be as eloquent and put together as Sable was, the Tigress finally gave up. Dropping to her knees, she opened her mouth one more time and let her heart do the talking.

"Yes. Absolutely, unequivocally, with all my heart, yes." Watching as he slid the ring the rest of the way onto her finger, she went on much to everyone's surprise. "Will you, Sable Lauder, be not only my Mate and the love of my life but also a true partner? Remembering that I'm not the 'little woman' who needs to be taken care of or pampered?" Leaning forward, so close she could feel his breath on her lips, she added, "There is no one in this whole universe I want to spend my life with but you. So, can we do it together?"

Feeling his arms wrapped around her before it registered that he'd moved, Lore was being picked up and swung around as Sable's lips slammed to hers. Opening completely, never ever wanted there to be anything between them, for them to always be there each other, she felt his kiss in every fiber of her being.

Never wanting their embrace to end, wanting to be alone with her Dragon and show him how very much she loved him, Lore tore her lips from his and groaned aloud when an incredibly thick Scottish brogue interrupted, "Ar ye comin' in, ur hae ye decided tae dae thes all on yer oown?"

Glaring at Draco who was grinning from ear-to-ear with an annoying twinkle in his eye, Lore grumbled, "We're coming, ya' grumpy old Dragon."

"That's Mr. Grumpy Auld Dragon tae ye, Lassie."

As everyone around them burst out laughing, Lore gave Sable one more hard-and-fast kiss before whispering, "See ya' in a minute, Dragon Man."

"Not if I see you first."

The heat of his gaze followed her all the way across the courtyard, where she promptly received a scolding from Jewel. "Whit exactly did ye think ye waur daein', yoong Lassie? Yoo're nae supposed tae be makin' it wi' yer Mate afair th' ceremony an' ye receive yer mark.'"

Deciding to take full advantage of it being her special day,

Lore rolled her bottom lip out as far as it would go while giving the Nymph her best sad-eyed look. Letting her chin fall to her chest, she looked up through her lashes, and while just barely keeping herself from laughing, she mock sniffed, "I just haaaad to see him, Auntie Jewel."

Laughing so hard that she had to lay her hand on Annika's shoulder to keep from tripping, she added, "I looooooove him."

Making a shooing motion with her hands as her shoulders shook with barely contained laughter herself, Jewel swatted Lore on the behind as she teased, "Mah puir laddie is in fur a lifetime ay trooble frae ye, ye bad lass."

"That and then some," Sydney, Minka, and Annika all chuckled in unison.

"You know it," the Tigress cheered. "I'm gonna keep him well-loved and on his toes.

Stopping at the massive wooden doors, intricately hand-carved with the symbol for each of the races represented by the Oracles, the shield of the Dragons front and center and by far the largest, Lore waited as Shavon laid her hand on one handle and Sydney the other. Trying to calm the butterflies in her tummy and the pounding of her heart, she was shocked when it was Sydney who spoke.

"Lore Bransfield, today you mate the one man in all the world made for just you by the Universe. May you and your Dragon know only the happiness of ages, the love of true Mates, and a lifetime of joy."

"Thank you." Her voice was barely a whisper as suddenly everything became very real. Looking at each of the ladies, she smiled with all the love in her heart and nodded, "I'll never be able to express how much I love each and every one of you and how thankful I am for everything."

Kissing her on one cheek while Annika kissed her on the

other, Minka snickered, "I've got a list of ways you can make it up to me."

Laughing as she stayed where she was while everyone else filed into the Citadel, Lore took a deep breath and as she let out, whispered, "Thank you, Mom and Dad, for showing me what real love is and what a gift waiting for my one true love could be. I hope I can be half the parent to my kids, if I ever get that far, that you were to me. I love you both."

Hearing the sound of boot heels striking the stone floors, she knew it was time for her to go. Thank the Goddess for Shavon, she'd made sure Lore was well prepared and knew her cues.

Opening the door, she could feel the majesty and importance of the fantastic fortress she was entering, but she only had eyes for her Dragon. Standing at the front of the Cathedral with the sun shining through an absolutely magnificent stained-glassed window stood Sable.

It was then she noticed how much like a Knight of the Round table he looked in his deep gray surcoat, form-fitting black pants, and knee-high super shiny boots. The Dragon so perfectly stitched across his chest was an exact duplicate of Herne donning the granite scales she herself had been blessed enough to wear.

Eyes meeting his, she felt the weight of his love-filled gaze to the very bottom of her soul. Holding tight to the single red rose he'd left on her pillow, she mouthed, "I love you," as she took one step after the other.

Meeting her halfway, something Lore knew was not in the original plans, she was just about to ask what was up when Sable whispered, "I just can't wait."

Ever so carefully picking her up, her Dragon cradled her in his arms and in the span of a single heartbeat was putting her feet on the floor in front of the altar. It was then she realized that Carrick, Draco, Creed, and Shavon were not in the very decorative, almost throne-like chairs sitting up on the dais.

Looking back to Sable who only smiled, her eyes were drawn to the sound of a door opening just over his shoulder. Watching as Creed, Carrick, Draco, Stone, and Gunnar filed in, she was just about to ask what was happening when the twelve-foot tall stained-glass window slowly opened from the middle.

Dumbfounded, wondering what could be happening, all her questions were answered when a breathtaking shining silver Dragon landed in the garden just outside the window. Folding his wings tight to his sides, the Winged Warrior walked forward, more graceful than she'd ever imaged a creature as large and dominating as he was could be and put his head and neck through the open window.

Eyes glued to his face, she could feel the magic and mysticism of the ages rolling off him in waves, but it was the lovely smile that curved his snout and the joy in his eyes that made her heart feel all the more lighter. Lowering his head until his eyes were as close to theirs as they could be, he began to speak telepathically to everyone in attendance.

"Welcome to this blessed place, Sable Lauder and Lorelei Bransfield. I am King Alarick. I am the first Dragon, the King responsible for the birth of the Dragon Guard, and the ruler who appointed Draco to be our Guardian, but on this very special day, I am only your humble servant. My heart is full to bursting for both of you and the love I feel in your presence."

Slowly moving his head from side to side, he went on, *"Not only are you the first couple to ever be mated in the Citadel but you, Sable, are the first Bearer ever to find his Mate."* Moving his head so that his left eye was looking right at her, he effused happiness as he said, *"Together, you and Lorelei will be the first couple in the history of Dragonkin, the Citadel, and the Oracles to jointly carry and protect our Rún Naofa. It speaks to your loyalty, integrity, and belief in all that we stand for that you are willing to hold the Truth of not only the Dragons, but of all creatures endowed with incredible abilities within your souls while never knowing what that Secret may be. We are forever in your debt. Should you ever have need of us, you have only to call."*

Clearing his throat, a rumble that seemed to emanate from all around them, he paused, the magic and intensity of his gaze making Lore wonder what was to come. Then he spoke, and her heart wanted to sing.

"For you, Sable and Lorelei, I have only this blessing. Written by a dear friend of mine, Shaman Lorelei Ashevak, let these beautiful words be the guiding light for eternity together."

Gasping at the sound of her grandmother's name, Lore held even tighter to Sable's hands as tears of sheer happiness slid down her cheeks.

"You, my beloved children, will feel no rain, for in each other's arms you will find the shelter that you need. May you be the warmth for one another that keeps the cold winds at bay. Never lonely, never wanting, you are two halves of the same whole."

"Two hearts that beat as one, two minds in perfect sync, two souls that strive for harmony, you come together in one life with common purpose and love. May beauty surround you both in the miraculous journey ahead, and joy fill every day of every year for your forever. May happiness be your constant companion and your days on earth and in the Heavens know no end."

"Treat yourselves and each other with respect. Always remind yourselves of what brought you together and keeps you in love. Tenderness, gentleness, and kindness are essential and what your love needs to grow and flourish. Even when times are tough, focusing on what is right and good between you will help you ride out every storm."

"You were made for one another. You were created by the Universe to be the perfect complement one to the other. You are the embodiment of the Faith, Love, and Hope the Great Mother has for

all her children. It is with all the love a grandmother can give her granddaughter and the Dragon with whom she will spend her life that I write these words."

"Always remember my dear sweet Lore, when you look up at the night sky, there are not stars but instead, holes where the light of my love is shining down on you and yours."

Leaning into Sable, loving that he anticipated her needs and put his arm around her, holding her close, she whispered, "How could she have known?"

Kissing the top of her head, Sable's voice drifted through her mind, *"Because she loves you and always will."*

Wanting to ask how he was so confident, Lore's thoughts were washed away when King Alarick spoke aloud, the rolling r's and lovely lilt of his Scottish accent filling every inch of the enormous cathedral. "May Dragon fire light your hearth. May Tiger eyes guard your path. May the Heavens always shine down upon you and the Universe guide you upon the path with no thorns."

Appearing on the podium beside the Dragon King's snout, Carrick, dressed in a surcoat of bright flaming red, smiled first at her and then at Sable before congratulating, "All the blessing to both of you, Lore and Sable. May you live long, fight hard, love harder, and have many children to flourish when their souls have gone to the heavens."

Winking at Lore, he stated, "The Granite Dragons were forged from the very fiber of the Universe and are known as Shield Dragons. They are protective to a fault, do not suffer fools nor the evil of lies. They are the Great Equalizers who possess a force that makes their adversaries with nefarious intentions quiver and shake. They use not only their minds but their hearts and experience when making all decisions. They love hard, strong, and endlessly. They never lose faith in whom or what they believe in. To mate a Granite Dragon means to accept all that they are and honor the power shared between Mates."

Turning to Sable, he gave a single nod. "White Tigers are the eternal symbol of courage, dignity, glory, and métier. They draw their strength from the great conviction they have in what they believe and who they love. They are true individuals with a uniqueness that draws others to them. The white of their fur signifies their comfort in the world of light or the spiritual realm. While their black stripes denote their ability to easily navigate the world of darkness or the physical plane. Protecting those they love is first and foremost, and a White Tigress will never bow to another to keep her family safe. To mate a White Tigress means to accept all that they are and honor the supremacy shared between Mates."

"It is my understanding that Sable has special plans for his and Lore's marking, so I have been instructed to tell all of you in attendance to retire to Sydney's home for dinner."

Turning towards Sable, Lore didn't even get to ask what was going on before he once again lifted her off the ground, held her lovingly to his chest and made a hasty exit as he whispered into her mind, *"I love you so much I think I might burst. Hold on, we're not going far."*

CHAPTER TWENTY-FIVE

"*Hold on, there's only one way to get there.*"
    "*Great! The Wind Walking Lauders hit the airwaves ...again.*"

Loving that she was already thinking of herself as a Lauder, Sable kissed the top of her head as he stepped into the portal Herne conjured. Stepping out onto the rolling, heather-covered hills of the Lauder ancestral home, he stood perfectly still until his Mate had settled.

"Open your eyes, *mo ghrá*," he breathed, using more of the Gaelic he'd spoken as a child. Slowly letting Lore's feet touch the ground, he waited for a reaction, anything to let him know he'd made the right decision.

Struck with fear, sure he'd screwed up what was to be not only the location of their honeymoon but their home, he almost jumped out of his skin when Lore spun on her toes, whooping, "A freakin' castle?"

Launching herself back into his arms, she rained kisses all over his face, jawline, and finally his lips as she continued to talk between pecks. "Oh...*kiss*... my...*kiss*... Goddess...*kiss*.

How...*kiss* did...*kiss* you...*kiss* know...*kiss*? How...*kiss* did...*kiss* you...*kiss* do...*kiss* this...*kiss*?

Reluctantly leaning his head back, needing not only to answer but also to clarify his Mate's first question, Sable snickered at the frown immediately appearing on Lore's face. "Hey! No fair! I was havin' fun!"

"Me, too. But let me ask, how did I know *what*?"

Eyes going from stormy to fanciful in the blink of an eye, she swooned, "Know that I always dreamt of having my honeymoon in a castle. Playing the Princess with my Prince charming." Once again furrowing her brow as she swatted his shoulder, his always-full-of-surprises Mate warned, "And if you ever tell anyone I said that I'll deny it and kick your ass just for good measure."

Giving her a mock shiver of fear, he winked and asked, "Would you like to live here? Forever?"

Mouth dropping open and eyes as big as saucers, Lore's hands softly clapped on both sides of her face right before she whispered conspiratorially, "Are you serious?"

"As Dragon fire and Tigress talons."

Kissing him soundly, his heart literally leaped in his chest as she shouted into his mind, *"Yes! Yes! Yes!"* Pulling back way too quickly, she looked him in the eye and with a tone that he'd learned she meant business, stated matter-of-factly, 'and remember, I said I love you before I knew you had a castle.'"

Laughing as freely as he could ever remember, Sable loosened his hold on Lore as she wiggled out of his arms. Landing on her feet, just as she always did, she grabbed his hand and started pulling, hollering over her shoulder, "Come on, I need a tour."

Commenting on the fantastic rock wall and the iron gate, she ooh'd and aah'd all the way through the garden, visions of he and Stone running through the flowers, his mother and Jewel scolding them for knocking blossoms off the bushes, and his father laughingly telling the ladies that 'boys will be boys'. Some of his best and happiest memories were spent on 'Lauder Island' as he and his twin called it, and he and Lore would create even more.

Forcing himself back to reality, he freely admitted, "All the refurbishing, replanting, and renovations were done courtesy of King Herne. He wanted to give us something special for the beginning of our lives together. Mom and Dad would've loved the thought of the old place being put to good use." Deciding their murders at the hands of Hunters was a tale for another time, he quickly rushed on, flooding their Mating bond with love and excitement.

Placing his hand on the door, he waggled his eyebrows, "I'm sure you noticed the old man plucked the names of your favorite flowers and images of gardens you'd tucked away from your memories to make it all the more special."

"Yeah, I knew he was up to something," she pretended to be annoyed.

"Well, flowers were just a small part."

Narrowing her eyes, he could tell his Tigress was trying to act suspicious, but the rapidly happy beat of her heart and her contagious scent of joy could not be contained. Placing the thumb and forefinger of his free hand under her chin, Sable lifted her head as he leaned down.

Meeting her in the middle, he gently laid his lips to hers and whispered into her mind, *"Le chèile bidh sinn a 'dol a-steach, gu bràth agus gu bràth, is tusa mo chridhe."*

"Together we enter, never to part, always and forever, you are my heart." The crack of Lore's voice as she repeated the phrase in English, the same verse Sable's father had used as he pledged an eternity of love to his mother all those centuries ago, made it hard for the Paladin to catch his breath.

Ending their kiss, he moved just enough to look into her

eyes as he said aloud, "Do you have any idea how much I love you, Lore Lauder?"

"Not near as much as I love you, Dragon Man, but you've got time to make it up to me."

Laughing right along with his Mate, Sable threw open the French doors, picked her up and carried her over the threshold. Stopping in the middle of the room his mother had always called her parlor, he was just about to set Lore down when she held on tighter and slammed her lips to his.

"Don't even think about it," her sassy command wove through his mind. *"The tour can come later, there's only one room I need to see right now."*

Needing no more motivation than the heat of her words and the scent of her arousal, Sable dashed to the first staircase he came to and took the stairs three at a time. Glad to see he hadn't forgotten the layout of the house, he stepped onto the third floor right outside the master suite and the place where he and Stone had collided when they were six resulting in matching head wounds and a week's worth of chopping wood in the bitter cold.

Kicking open the door and crossing the room without touching the floor, he let his Tigress do as she would. Captured in her gaze, never wanting to be anywhere but with her, his body caught fire as Lore slowly, torturously slid her body down his until her feet touched the floor.

Outlining his lips with the tips of her fingers, her voice a tantalizing blend of smoke and fire, and love and lust, she breathed, "You are so much better than any fantasy I ever had." Her fingers traced his jawline as her lips curled into a sensual smile that had his heart racing, and his Dragon humming with appreciation. "The past is the past and forever is ours. Thank you for believing in me. I love you, Sable Lauder, I love you with every single beat of my heart."

Unwilling to move, barely breathing, sure he was dreaming, or if not, that he would somehow ruin the most perfect moment of his very long life if he dared to utter a word, Sable stood utterly still. Forcing his eyes to stay open even as they fought to slide closed, his body shook with the sheer power it took to restrain himself when she slid her jaw along his and purred.

Reading her mind, the thoughts awash with excitement, adoration, love, and wanton need, his pride soared when Lore and her Tigress sighed in unison, *"Covered in our scent. Marked as our own."*

Running her hands down his body, doing the same with her fingertips as she'd done with her face, her body vibrated against his, the audible sound of her purring throwing gas on his already flaming desire. There was nothing he wouldn't do for her. Nothing he would ever hold back from her. Lore had saved him. Shown him the man he wanted to be. She was his everything, forever and always.

Unable to hold back any longer, enveloped in his want and her need, their desire to become one, Sable put his lips to hers. Summoning the invincible strength he'd been given by the Universe, he forced both himself and his Dragon to go slow, be gentle, savor every single second. He would do whatever it took to make this time, and every time, everything his Mate could ever want.

But of course, Lore had other ideas...

Gripping his shoulders, she pulled his body to her with an intensity and appetite that filled his heart and soul with an unbridled power he knew came from the union of their souls in every way possible. Letting her take the lead, Sable became her willing follower. Open to his Tigress, willing her to do as she wanted, assuring her that he was hers and *only hers*, he reined in his raging libido.

The longer she kissed and caressed, the more desire and longing she created, the harder it was for Sable to wait. Teasingly removing his surcoat then the long-sleeved black shirt, she kissed her way down his chest and across his torso, unbuttoning his trousers as she went.

Standing up and taking the tiniest of steps backward, she snapped her fingers as his pants fell over his boots and winked. A split-second later, Sable was completely undressed while his Mate's eyes gazed at his erection while she slowly licked her lips.

Moving quicker than even he knew he could, Sable slid his hands around Lore and lowered the zipper at the back of her gown. Slipping her out of the offending material as quickly as he could, his mouth watered at the sight of her hardened nipples pushing against the soft, white lace of her bra.

Body moving without the slightest recognition from his blood-deprived brain, he sucked first one and then the other into his mouth, teasing it with just the tip of his tongue. Savoring her taste, inhaling her scent, marking her just as she'd marked him, Sable continued until Lore was holding fistfuls of hair and saying his name again and again as if it were her own special mantra.

Laying her back on the bed, his eyes feasted on the beauty before him. Lifting her hips as his fingers slipped under the silk waistband of her panties, his cock hardened to nearly the point of pain when her hands skimmed her ribs making a beeline for the glistening curls at her center.

Up on the bed with his knees on either side of her thighs, the tip of his erection bumped her heated skin forcing a groan of desire from both of them. Needing to touch, to taste, to mark every inch of her, Sable put his palms on either side of her head.

Kissing across her chest, his mouth trailed straight back to her breast, nipping and sucking until Lore's moans of pleasure echoed off the stone walls. Following the rhythm of their rampaging hearts, he continued to taste every part of her body. She was intoxicating and addicting, igniting all his senses, bringing his body in complete harmony with hers.

He not only wanted her, he needed her, craved her, knew without Lore by his side, in his arms, in his heart and soul, the torture he'd suffered for centuries would be nothing compared to the pain of losing her. Completion, pure and simple, she was the only thing, the *only person* he would ever need.

Muttering his name over and over, louder and louder as her fingers dug into his scalp, she directed him, guided him, told him how to love her. Her thoughts beat at him, telling him how very much she wanted to wear his mark and for him to wear hers.

Needing to completely connect with the woman who'd driven the darkness from his mind, shone the light to his soul, slayed the demons of his past, Sable knew there was no holding back. With no other thought than feeling the warmth of her body wrapped around his painfully hard length, Sable acted on pure instinct.

Nerves, apprehension, all the fear of making a fool out of himself that he'd experienced before flew from his mind. All he had to do was stay in perfect commune with his Mate. Together, they would weave their own perfect future.

There was nothing like the feel of her body against his, no fragrance that could ever compare to the scent of her arousal filling his senses. His name on her lips, coupled with her feelings of unconditional love and unequivocal acceptance flowing through their mating bond created an incredibly heady combination forcing him to want nothing less than everything with his Tigress, but he had to be sure.

Shoving everything but his complete commitment to always put her needs before his, Sable stopped all movement. Lifting his head, a cheeky grin of pure male pride crossed his lips when she moaned at the loss of his body.

Laying his fingers upon her lips, he spoke with all the love in his heart, "Lore." When she didn't answer, only reached for him and lifted her hips, he fought his own desire and pulled farther away. "Lore," he barked the command making sure he was smiling when her eyes popped open.

Laying his hand on her cheek, he quickly kissed the tip of her nose before asking, "Are you sure? There's truly no rush. I love you, and I'll wait an eternity if that's what you need."

Licking his finger up one side and down the other, she sucked the digit into her mouth and answered directly into his mind, *"I have never been more sure of anything. Make me yours, Dragon Man."*

Needing no more encouragement, his lips slammed to hers in a scorching embrace of hunger and desire. Reminding himself to go slow. Forcing his Dragon to stay in the background, he tore his lips from hers.

Kissing along her jaw and down her neck, he tasted his way across the soft, sweet skin of her décolletage, paying special attention to the glorious valley between her breasts. Panting and mewling, unable to form a coherent word, Lore's back bowed off the bed as her short, manicured nails dug into his shoulders. Undeterred, wanting her more with every beat of his heart, he teased the silken skin of her stomach with tiny love bites, a preview of the marking that was to come.

Finally, reaching the glistening curls covering her pussy, he gently spread her legs. Laying butterfly kisses on the inside of her thighs, he placed one and then the other of her legs over his shoulders. Needing to taste her, to take in her very essence, he was driven to make Lore's first time the best it could possibly be. Only she mattered. His needs were inconsequential.

Whispering into her mind at precisely the same time that he slowly pushed his middle finger through her curls and into the warmth of her body, he promised, *"No matter where or when, you will always be my first, middle, and last concern. I love you, mo Thíogair"*

The thrashing of her head and tightening of her legs around his neck as he pushed farther into her tight wet pussy spurred him on to add a second finger right alongside the first. Making a come-hither motion with his middle finger, he tickled the sensitive bundle of nerves deep in her body that he instinctively knew would set her on fire.

Her receptiveness to his touch was amazing. The feel of her body as he loved her with his digits was mind-blowing. In that very moment, there was no doubt in Sable's mind that he'd found Heaven. Then she climaxed, and there was no doubt he could die in that very moment a very, *very* happy man.

Screaming his name and pulling his hair, she went on and on, her juices wetting his hand from only his fingers alone. Slipping his fingers from her, his tongue instantly took its place. Licking and tasting, pushing her higher, he felt another orgasm racing to its glorious end before the first had ebbed.

Wanting...*needing* her to orgasm again, he rubbed her swollen, throbbing clit between his thumb and forefinger as he thrust his tongue in and out of her, just barely touching the proof of her virginity. Heels digging into his back, her keens reverberated off the walls as again and again she came into his mouth and onto his beard.

Eating at her, needing to have every drop of her essence within him, the contraction of her body began to slow. Her breathing returned to normal. Her body relaxed. She sighed, and the sound was quite literally music to his ears.

Running the tip of his tongue along her outer lips, he lapped up the very last drop of her essence before once again kissing the inside of both of her thighs. Raising his head, the breath was stolen from his lungs as he looked at the one and only woman in all the world who he knew beyond all doubt would love him no matter what.

Laying before him with her head thrown back, her lips seductively curved in a lazy smile, and her breasts gently rising and falling in the sweetest sign of completion he could ever imagine. Lore was nothing short of absolutely magnificent, and she was all his.

Rising to his knees, he kissed his way up her body, nipped along her neck to her ear and whispered, "Together...always and forever."

Inch by mind-blowing inch, he slid into the woman the Universe had made for him. Little by little, he stopped to let her body adjust to his size. A feeling unlike anything he'd ever imagined exploded within every fiber of his being.

Nothing had ever felt so right...*so perfect*. Sable was right where he was meant to be and come what may he would never leave. Reaching Lore's maidenhead, stopping instantly, he laid his lips to hers. Pouring all the love and adoration he felt for her into that one single kiss, he whispered into her mind, *"You are my sun, moon, and stars and I will spend every day of forever showing you how very much you mean to me."*

Deepening their kiss as he pressed through the tender boundary within, Sable was utterly blown away by Lore's strength when she barely winced at his intrusion. Holding both he and his Mate absolutely still, his body celebrated the feel of her inner walls welcoming him.

Chest swelling with pride when her sigh of pleasure echoed his, he could have flown without wings at the feel of her arousal building, her body needing...*wanting* what only *he* could give her. Moving before he could, Lore rolled her hips, her inner muscles massaging him, pushing him, forcing him to move with her.

Her fingers, now on his back, ran up and down his spine. Her legs wound tight around his waist. He could feel her everywhere. They were one as it was always meant to be. The perfection of the moment was nothing short of inexplicable. Gutted, completely and irrevocably under Lore's spell, Sable felt the final missing piece of his very being snap into place.

Looking up at him, her radiant smile brightening the entire room, the touch of her hand to his face drove what few coherent thoughts he had left from his mind. Matching the hypnotic rhythm of her erotic dance thrust for thrust, he would never want for anything ever again. Hearts beating as one, the perfect syncopation of what Fate and Destiny had put into place at the beginning of time, Sable was completely surprised when Lore sexily ordered, "Bring on the fire, my very own Dragon Man."

Helpless but to do anything short of completely and totally pleasing his Mate, Sable pulled back, held perfectly still for half a heartbeat then thrust back into his Tigress until their hips collided and she wailed his name. Unable to control his passion for a second longer, driven by the magnitude of Lore's need flooding through their mating bond, he thrust in and out of his Mate with a furious tempo she met head-on.

Higher and higher their hunger grew, the need to be one so intense, so demanding that for the first time ever Sable gave up complete control. Holding nothing back, all he'd ever been, all he was, and all he could ever be burst wide open for his one and only. From that moment forward, for all eternity, he and Lore would be one. No one and nothing, not even the demons of the past could ever tear them apart.

Reaching between their bodies, his need for them to climax together being his only focus, Sable tenderly pinched her clit between his thumb and forefinger giving one final, powerful thrust. Roaring their completion to the Heavens as one, moving together, loving one another in the extraordinary way only true fated Mates can, he felt a twinge followed by a flash of fire on the side of his neck. Eyes flying open at the sound of Lore's sharp gasp, he watched the brilliant marking appear on her neck and knew he wore its exact match.

Unable to look away from the perfect set of Dragon flames emblazed with the stripes of his Mate's Tigress blooming right over the beat of her jugular, the awe Lore felt at watching his Mating mark appear filled their Mating bond. Gazing adoringly at each other, their adoration and commitment growing even more, the couple floated back to earth, each more fulfilled than they could have ever imagined.

Holding Lore close, waiting for his heart to stop racing and his brain to start working, Sable leisurely maneuvered their satiated bodies towards the head of the bed. Once they were comfortable, he was perfectly content to lay with Lore in his arms and listen to her sleep.

Hours later, when the last rays of the sun were disappearing from the open windows, he smiled slyly as her breathing changed, and she started to move. When she finally lifted her head and propped her chin on her hand where it lay upon his chest, he kissed her soundly before handing her a rectangular gray velvet box.

Popping up, he loved the freedom she already felt in his presence as she didn't bother to cover her stunning body as she scolded, "This is so not fair. I haven't even given you one present, and you're giving me a third?"

"Third?"

"Yes. My ring..." She held up her hand and flittered her fingers. "The castle..." She tilted her head to the side and raised her eyebrows before laughing out loud, "Okay, that was for both of us." Lifting the box, she added, "But I'm guessing this is just for me."

"And you would be right." Winking, he insisted, "Now, open it before I do it for you."

"Okay, okay, okay." Opening the box, she gasped, "Oh, Sable... I mean...wow! Just wow!"

Reaching in the box, she lifted the tennis bracelet he'd had made by a Mate of one of the Guardsmen from Carrick's Clan. A single row of black diamonds elegantly mounted between two rows of white diamonds with three bells made from the scales of his Dragon attached at the lobster-claw clasp.

Taking the bracelet from Lore's trembling hand, he lovingly laid it on the top of her wrist before securing the clasp just under the rapidly beating pulse underneath. Looking into her eyes, he ever-so-slightly moved her hand up and down just enough for the bells to melodically ring.

Unable to stand even the scant distance between them, he pulled Lore into his lap, kissed the tip of her nose and while looking deep into her eyes, beamed as he once again made the bells on her bracelet jingle, "Guess what it means when a bell is ringing?"

Throwing her arms around his neck, she gave him a quick kiss, before giggling with excitement, "No clue. Tell me."

Kissing her again, this time with every ounce of love in his heart, he answered directly into her mind, *"It means a Dragon is kissing his Mate."*

Returning his love and affection with more of her own, Lore's chuckled response served to reinforce exactly why she was absolutely perfect for him, *"Well, I sure hope they made lots of extras, 'cause we're gonna be wearin' this set out by the end of the week."*

Until we meet again...

EPILOGUE

*B*ang! Bang-Bang-Bang!

Racing into the hallway and down the first staircase she came to, Lore ended up sliding down the newly polished banister as she yelled, "Stop that racket! You're gonna break down my new door!"

Getting ready to launch herself onto the floor, she ended up squealing, "Watch out below!"

Turning on a dime, Sable threw out his arms at the ready, catching her as if it was something they'd practiced a hundred times. "Way to make an entrance, my love."

"Good catch, Dragon Man." She kissed him quickly. "I am loving the new banisters."

"I can tell," he teasingly scoffed just as the banging resumed.

Side-by-side, in step the whole way, Lore stood to the side as her Mate opened the door and growled, "What the fuck, Stone?" Whipping her head to the side to check for knuckle marks, she glared before warning, "Damn good thing there are no marks. I'm still good and pissed that my Clinic looks like a friggin' bomb went off in it."

Holding his index finger at the same time Gunnar and two other Dragons she did not know appeared, her Mate's twin kind of apologized, "Sorry, but I gotta talk to Sable."

Giving her brother-in-law an eye-roll followed by her best Vanna White hand motion towards her Dragon, she sarcastically bubbled, "Stone meet Sable." Winking at her one true love, she went on, "Sable, I'd like to introduce you to your blockhead brother."

Laughing just like she knew he would, Sable grabbed her hand and pulled her to him as he opened the door wider and invited, "Come on, the whole damn lot of ya'."

Swooning just a little bit every time she looked at him, it didn't hurt that the longer they stayed in Scotland, the stronger her Mate's brogue became. It was sexy in a way that made her feel like the Maiden in the castle waiting for her roguish Knight to come and rescue her.

Snapping out of one of her favorite daydreams, she was whapped right in the face with a cloud of rage, frustration, and pissed off Dragon Paladin that had her blurting out, "Who pissed in y'all's Cheerios?"

Doing an about-face so fast he was nothing but a blur. Stone stopped, took a step forward, and held up his cell phone. Looking at the picture, it took a second for her to react but not Sable.

Voice low and rumbly, the scent of burning cherry wood filled her senses. Her Mate was mad, no, check that, he was downright furious and heading towards Warrior Dragon at a high rate of speed.

Putting two and two together, Lore finally recognized that the image was of Creed after the holy hell had been beat right out of him. "What the..."

"Who?" Sable snarled, cutting off her question.

Swiping his finger across the screen, Stone shoved the screen closer.

"XOXO Assassin," Lore read the computer-generated note aloud. "What the hell? He signed the ransom note with hugs and kisses?"

Turning towards his Lore, Sable laid his hands on her shoulders before leaning down until they were eye-to-eye. "It's not a he. It's a she," he seethed. "And it's not a ransom note, it's a warning. Creed has twenty-four hours to live.

ASSASSIN

Coming Summer 2019

MEET STONE AND ANNIKA

(I promise they'll *blast* their way into your heart!)
DRAGON HER HOME

CHAPTER ONE

"Well, this is a fine mess you've gotten yourself into," he grumbled to himself, fighting the threat of frostbite and silver poisoning with the minuscule magic he could cobble together. "Why didn't I pay more attention when mom and grandma were trying to teach me how to draw enchantment from the Earth."

"Because you were young and foolish and continued to tell them that you had a Dragon King, and you knew better."

"Yeah, well, see where that's gotten me," he sighed. "I'm freezing my ass off in a frozen wasteland and having a conversation with my dead twin."

"The memory of your dead twin," the vision of Sable corrected with a chuckle. *"Neither one of us knows what I would've looked like by now."*

"Exactly like me, just like you did when we were born and just like you did when you..."

"Disappeared? Died?" The shadowy image shook its head. *"You can say the words. Hell, you just did. Not saying them now, denying the truth when it's staring you in the face, won't make it all any less real."*

"Yeah, I know..." Unable to look at the specter anymore, he diverted his eyes and added, "I need to focus." And just like that, the manifestation of the memory of his one and only brother was gone.

"Alright, Asshole. Time to get your shit together. Figure out what's going on and get the hell outta here." Still looking at the same broken piece of wood poking through the snow, he growled, "I can't be losing my mind. I refuse to lose my mind. I know what I felt. It was *not* my imagination." Slamming his fist against the icy boards, he snarled, "And it's still out there. I know it is. Humming, clawing, pulsating...calling to me like a flame calls to a moth."

Something or some*one*, a magical vacuum, an unconceivable vortex of untold mysticism was literally sucking the life-force given to all of the Universe's chosen Warriors from his veins like wretched vermin pulling marrow from the bones of its kill, and the son of a bitch simply refused to let up. At first, in Stone's semi-conscious state after the first of the beatings, he'd thought there was another Dragon nearby. A magic – warm, familiar – like calling to like, a Siren's song in a sea of pain. Reaching out to make contact, the ancient mysticism of his Dragon King was ripped from his soul, and for his trouble, the Guardsman was metaphorically whipped with a cat-o-nine-tails that left all too real gashes and blood covering his back.

"I'll find that bastard. I'll find him, and he'll pay for betraying one of his own..."

Painstakingly climbing to his feet, he faced the wall, counted to three while inhaling as deeply as possible with five broken ribs, and in one powerful motion slammed his dislocated shoulder back into place. Thankfully, the loud clang of his silver chains and the bone-jarring rattle of his shackles overshadowed the gritted-teeth groan that escaped his lips. Panting, trying to stay upright, he gagged as the coppery taste of blood coated his mouth and flowed down his throat.

"Way to go, Dumbass," he berated himself. "More blood loss is exactly what you need. Biting your tongue, huh? Yeah, you're one of the best all right. Swift move, Loser."

Laying his throbbing shoulder against the frozen rocks, he prayed for the excruciating pain to subside. Sleep was what he needed most, to slip into the healing slumber required by all Guardsmen to repair the extensive damage his captors had inflicted upon him. Unfortunately, it was a chance he simply couldn't take.

Known for using their enemies' weaknesses against them. The Overlords were barbaric. They were patient motherfuckers, watching, and waiting for any slipup, any lapse in judgment – no matter how small – that they could exploit for their own brutal ends.

Letting his guard down for even a single second would result in death or worse. Of that, there was no doubt. "After all, that's how these nasty sons of whores got the jump on me in the first place," he growled under his breath. "And how many fucking days ago was that?"

Staring out the cracked window of the three-sided shack they'd thrown him into after each and every beating, he passed the time dreaming up new and inventive ways of stringing that fucking Matchmaker up by her perfectly manicured red fingernails. Sure, she was only four-foot-eleven and looked like someone's well-to-do Grandmother, but she was smart, cunning, and damned near as resilient as the Universe Herself...probably as old.

"Wish I could figure out *what* she really was? Right now, all bets are on the evil sister of the Wicked Witch of the West..."

What the hell was she thinking? Demanding he make a trip of this magnitude on his own – with no backup of any kind. "It wouldn't surprise me if all of this horse shit was part of her grand plan." He'd heard from more than one person talk about the extreme lengths she'd go to when putting a male in the path of his true Fated Mate.

But Creed said Gerri wasn't the pain in the ass everyone made her out to be, and there was no one Stone trusted more than his long-time friend. Still, he'd fought and argued until the very last second.

"You're really gonna take orders from Gerri freakin' Wilder? That's who we are now? A bunch of whipped Lizards?"

Although Creed didn't turn away from the window, Stone knew there was a scowl on the Commander's face by the fire in his retort. "No. I am helping out a friend and powerful ally who has requested our assistance."

"And you don't think it's weird that she specifically asked for me and only me?"

"No." The single word answer might as well have been a punch to the face. Slowly turning around, ominous music blaring in the Guardsman's head, Creed Mathers, the oldest Guardsman/Dragon/man Stone had ever met who was also the Leader, Commander, and Elder of the Paladins took a deep, measured breath before glaring a hole directly through Stone's forehead.

"No?" Stepping forward, the Guardsman's tone dropped an octave as the heat of his Dragon's fire rose in his throat. "That's all you're gonna say? You expect me to blindly do what she wants? What was her excuse? Was it at least worth the risk?"

"No, I expect you to do as you're told...as you're ordered." Pausing for less than a second, he went on, "She didn't give one." Holding out his arm with the palm of his hand facing front, the unequivocal gesture for 'shut your mouth, I'm not finished, and you are damn good and well going to stand there and listen,' Stone's Commander, mentor, and most of all, friend, took a seat. Laying his hands atop the massive mahogany desk he'd carved with his very own talons almost three millennia ago, Creed looked up and added, "And I didn't ask. Someone

needs our help. That's who we are. It's what we do. No questions asked."

"But..."

"But we are Paladins." The last word brought to life by the fervent conviction in his voice simply could not be ignored. "There is no choice. It is more than a calling – it is who we are. The blood that runs through our veins and the magic that fills every fiber of our beings is a mere conception brought to life by the will of the Universe. By our very existence, we are a testament to the belief that justice must prevail. To question our duty, our mission, the reason for our existence – is to shame our Kind."

"I know who I am." Even to his own ears, his voice sounded too rough, too wild, too...Dragon.

"Do you?" Creed challenged. "Or have you gotten soft?"

"My purpose is clear." Clenching his fists so tightly droplets of his life's essence dripped through his fingers as the flat edges of his nails bit into his palms, Stone ground out, "I know who and what I am."

"Then act like it," Creed pushed through gritted teeth. "In the air in thirty. Reports every two hours."

The 'discussion' was over. Sure, Stone could've bitched and moaned and ended up with a broken jaw for his trouble. It had happened before. Was bound to happen again – just not then.

Thankfully, Hilgar, the Ancient Dragon who'd chosen Stone as his own, put a stop to anything foolhardy the Guardsman had in mind. Visions of flying thousands of miles while trying to heal broken bones flashed vividly in his mind. Then to make sure he didn't forget, the Dragon King instantly set every single one of Stone's nerve-endings on fire just long enough to ensure complete and utter compliance.

That simple reminder of what it was like to soar the skies in subzero weather while injured had been enough – and would not be forgotten anytime soon. Stomping off, the

Guardsman packed his go-bag and headed for the farthest field.

Donning his granite scales as the last ray of the sun fell behind the mountains, he gave a single mighty thrust of his wings and shot into the skies. Ignoring the calls of his Brethren, refusing to explain, Stone closed off all communication and made a beeline for the coldest, back-ass, hole in the gods-forsaken earth - the Qikiqtaaluk Region.

Hours passed, with every mile the temperature plummeted, and the winds howled. Simmering anger and bone-deep weariness caused him to drop his guard and proceed on autopilot somewhere in the darkest hours of the night.

Searing pain gashed his underbelly...

Blazing bolts of black magic lit the sky in every direction...

Fighting to stay airborne, his wings froze in mid-thrust...

And that's the last memory he had, until...

Waking up in shackles, the sharp, silver tip of an Overlord's boot battering his ribs, Stone had reached for Hilgar and the strength only the Dragon King could give him. Coming up empty-handed and utterly alone, he did the only thing he could do...*survive*.

READ THE WHOLE STORY HERE!

Also Part of the Kindle Unlimited Library!

MEET ABE

Big, Bald, and bad to the bone, he leaves 'em all in the dust!

Tattooed, dark-eyed, and 7'2" this Dragon makes Hell's Angels look like soccer moms at the spa and turns the bad guys to ash!!!

Back the heck off or pay the price. At least that was the plan...

Then a severed head was delivered to a certain fiery redhead and all bets were off.

Fate is working overtime to keep this couple safe, but it's gonna take one heckuva SAVAGE to save the day!

CHAPTER ONE

"Where's the stiff and how'd he die?"

"The *victim,*" the Dragon Protection Agency's Pathologist ground out through gritted teeth, making Abe raise the right side of his mouth in a shit-eating grin. Teasing her was always the highlight of going to a crime scene. "...is female and she's this way." Raising her gloved hand, Dr. Kelsey Whittingham motioned to the black body bag sitting on the edge of grass. "I prefer..."

"You prefer *not* to work with me, Doc," Abe chuckled, knowing it wasn't true but pushing his luck. "But Gil calls the shots. So, let's get this over with as quickly as we can."

Stepping in front of him, a hard feat in and of itself since he was seven-feet tall with long legs and *always* moving at a high rate of speed, the six-foot-three Valkyrie spun on her toes and stopped. Holding up the index finger of her right hand, she cleared her throat and in what Abe called her Dr. Death voice, thick with her original Norwegian accent, deadpanned, "Number one, I do not have a preference with concern to who attends any incident. *You* are as good as any other agent." Adding her middle finger to the mix, she continued, "Number two, you *will* show respect to the dead at *my* crime scene." Raising her ring finger, she added, "Number three, *you* don't scare me. I can and *will* kick your ass if you piss me off." Pointing all three fingers right at his chest, she gave him one single stab before plastering on a fake smile and nodding, "Now, play nice. We have company coming."

"Wait. What?" Knowing damn good and well that Kelsey loved fucking with him more than drinking single malt whiskey and playing darts - it was the beauty of their friendship, Abe refused to let her see him sweat. Sure, he hated anyone that wasn't part of his team being at a crime scene before he'd been able to scope it out for himself, but the way Dr. Death had said 'company' had both he and his Dragon preparing for the worst.

Pushing his hands into the special-order, XXXL black latex gloves he always carried in the pocket of his black leather jacket, the Guardsman squatted beside the body bag. Paying close attention to every single detail as Myles, one of the DPA's EMTs who also worked with Kelsey when needed, slowly pulled the zipper down, he caught the familiar scent of Wolf, cauterized skin, and liquid silver.

Holding out his hand for the EMT to pause when he saw that the victim had been decapitated, his eyes shot to Kelsey. "Have you swabbed? Can I touch?"

"Yes, and Yes." She gave a single nod. "She's all yours until the bus gets here."

Focus back on the body, he ran the pad of his index finger along the incision at the base of her head. "Smooth. Surgical. Precise," he murmured to himself as he moved to the blackened skin ringing the top of the victim's neck. "This one, too." Without looking up, he nodded to Myles, "Okay, show me more. Stop at her waist."

Taking mental notes as he continued to talk to himself,

Abe listed off, "Still dressed. Only a few drops of blood on her shoulders and the top of her collar. Whatever was used instantly cauterized the wound."

"Had to be damned near flaming." Pointing to the top of the spine, Myles went on, "See how the bone's burnt, too?"

Not looking away from the corpse, Abe slowly nodded.

"The blade had to be heated to somewhere between fourteen-hundred and eighteen-hundred degrees Fahrenheit. Not to mention, razor sharp and swung with incredible force." Clearing his throat, the silver and white Dragon who knew more about anatomy and physiology than nearly anyone in the world, added, "Sound like anyone we know?"

"Not anyone. Everyone," Abe grunted, trying to work some levity and failing. "But, there's no scent of the assailant. *No* one we know would be able to hide their scent from us."

"You're thinkin' too close to home."

Leaning his ass onto the heels of his well-worn cowboy boots and laying his elbows on the top of his thighs, Abe narrowed his eyes and prompted, "Enlighten me, Professor."

"And if you say a Valkyrie, I promise I won't take offense," Kelsey sarcastically interjected, her lavender eyes swirling with the promise of retribution.

"No scent," Myles reiterated before moving right along without acknowledging the Valkyries not-so-veiled threat. "Had to be a Reaper. It's the only thing that makes sense."

"Okay," Abe considered. "Let's say you're right. Mind you, I don't think you are, but for the sake of argument, let's take your theory all the way. How do you explain the rips in the top of her blouse that go all the fucking way through the flesh of her ti...*ahem*, I mean breasts," he quickly corrected, not wanting anymore shit from Dr. Death. "And the three buttons..." He pointed directly to the place on the silken fabric where the first buttons should have been. "...that should be right here but have been torn off?" Pausing for a split-second for effect, he picked right up where he'd left off. "All of that tells me that whoever or *whatever* did this had one helluva set of claws and ripped something from around her neck. Reapers snatch their victims from the side or behind. Do not behead until they get them underground. Witnesses are not their thing. And, those sick bastards never take trophies." Slapping his hand on his leg, he nodded, "And the mother fucker would did this most definitely took something for himself."

"How ya' figure?" Both the Dragon and the Valkyrie asked in unison.

"Because every damned thing points to here." Touching the body at the base of what was left of the neck, he explained, "See? No marks. No scratches. Nothing at all in this little circle." Glancing at Kelsey and then Myles, he added, "I'd bet you a thousand dollars and a year's worth of beer that she was wearing a necklace with a pendant and the evil bastard snatched it off her neck right before he relieved her of her head."

"Well, shit, as much as I hate to admit it, you might just be right," the Valkyrie cautiously agreed. "We'll do a spectrograph on it to see if there's any bruising not associated with being decapitated under the skin and in the musculature."

"Yeah, sure, you do you, Doc. I understood exactly none of that gobbledygook."

"But," Myles jumped in. "If what you're sayin' is really what happened. Not only was our bad guy this close to her..." He held his palm less than a foot from the tip of the dead girl's nose. "He was also faster than anyone I've ever met. This bastard surprised an Alpha female during a full moon, ripped off her necklace, and decapitated her well before she even thought about getting her claws or fangs out."

"Okay, unzip this bag the rest of the way and let's see

what else we find." Eyes glued to the body, Abe reverently asked, "Was she mated?"

"No, only marked as an Alpha." Lifting her left arm, Myles showed him the flaming moon brand on the underside of her wrist.

"Refresh my memory..." He pointed at the glyph. "That means she's Alpha, high ranking within her Pack, but not the Leader, yeah?"

"Yes, that's correct," Myles answered. "She's also relatively young for an Alpha considering the Flaming Moon Pack has an incredibly deep hierarchy and the only way anyone reaches Alpha level is by blood sport."

"Ya' gotta love the old ways," Abe sighed. "How old is she, anyway?"

"Only forty." Kelsey shook her head. "At forty years from birth, Valkyries are still considered teenagers. I can't imagine losing a sister so early in her life."

"Neither can I."

The words reached his ears just as the heavenly scent of roses, lavender, and chocolate-covered cherries forced him up onto his feet. Turning so quickly it took his vision a second to focus, suddenly punch-drunk, woozy, and way out of his depth.

Holding out his hand, his entire world was turned upside-down and inside-out the moment her hand touched his, but it wasn't until she said, "Agent Sera Morningside. I hear we're going to be partners."

SAVAGE PROTECTOR

COMING SUMMER 2019

GET THE SCOOP ON SYDNEY RIGHT HERE

Twenty-four-hour shifts were going to be the death of her, especially when they lasted almost thirty. Of course, she had no one to blame but herself. She could've said no when Dr. Monoghan asked her to assist with an appendectomy. "No" had been on the tip of her tongue until she caught sight of the messy blonde curls spilling over the pillow as her mentor pointed towards their patient. She *knew* this was one she couldn't ignore. Monoghan's entire surgical team was male and very good at their chosen professions. Unfortunately, they knew how good they were, which resulted in a collective bedside manner that totally sucked. There was no way the little tow-headed sprite she'd heard singing would've been able to relax in the presence of the massive amounts of testosterone they spewed.

Grabbing her thirteenth cup of coffee of the day, Sam prayed for no complications and headed in to see her patient. Nothing could've prepared her for the innocent blue eyes surrounded by long thick lashes, topping the cutest little chubby cheeks in the world that looked up at her as she knocked on the half closed door. For a second, she thought of another pair of azure eyes that heated her from the inside out and promised hot, sweaty nights spent satiating each other's needs.

Shaking her head to clear her thoughts, she walked to the end of the bed and grabbed the chart. "Hi, Sydney, I'm Dr. Malone. You can call me Dr. Sam."

The sweet girl giggled. "Sam's a boy's name."

"You're right," she smiled. "Unless it's a nickname for Samantha."

Visibly relaxing for the first time since Sam had entered the room, her patient answered, "Oh, that makes sense. There was a Samantha at my old school, but we never called her Sam, she wanted to be called Samantha...Samantha Jane." Sydney thought for a moment. "Sam sure would've been easier."

"It sure would've been," the young doctor agreed, winking at the obviously intelligent child before her. "Did you recently change schools?" She looked towards the woman sitting in the chair, who continued to mess with her cell phone, basically ignoring the child in the hospital bed. It seemed the opportune time for the adult in the room to speak up, but apparently, the woman hadn't gotten the memo. When said "adult" didn't even look up, Sam checked the file, not surprised to find that the woman was a social worker, *not* a family member. Sam and Sydney were definitely on their own for this exam.

Probably easier that way....

"It says here you have a tummy ache." She pointed to the chart she still held. "Can you show me exactly where it hurts?"

"Right here." Sydney placed her little chubby hands across her midsection and scrunched up her nose. "But I really just want to go home."

"Now, Sydney, you know the doctor in the emergency

room said you need an operation," the woman in the chair stated in a flat, irritating tone, finally entering the conversation, but still not glancing up.

The thought of smacking the woman danced through Sam's coffee-soaked brain. She wondered if *that* would get some kind of reaction from her. Instead of acting on her thoughts, the young doctor turned just in time to see Sydney's eyes fill with tears. Before the first one could fall, Sam asked, "Have you ever been in a hospital before?"

As soon as it was out of her mouth, she wished it back. She knew better. You never asked a ward of the state that question when you didn't know the whole story. What a rookie mistake, one she wouldn't have made had she not been so incredibly frustrated with the woman to her right. The next thing she heard simultaneously broke her heart and filled her with pride.

"Yes, Dr. Sam, I was in the hospital the day the big truck hit our car." Sydney continued in an unwavering tone, merely explaining the facts, all traces of her previous weakness gone. "Mommy and Daddy went to Heaven, and I went to live in the 'big house' with all the other kids. Miss Crutchfield...," Sydney looked over at the woman and rolled her little eyes, "she's my social worker. I have no aunties or uncles, and my nana and pop pop are already in Heaven. It's okay where I live, but I really wish I could go back to my old school to see my friends."

Sam counted to ten in her head, battling her anger, and returned her focus to her patient. Sydney was a tough little girl and one smart cookie. The child went on to tell Sam that the accident had happened about six months ago, and she was waiting to go live with a foster family. She spoke like a miniature adult, using all the correct terms and stating the facts of her situation with detached accuracy while she was examined.

The fact that *the child* was sharing the information and the useless state employee was busy with an inanimate object caused Sam's barely controlled anger to boil again. Why the hell did people with no interest in caring for children become social workers? Shouldn't they at least care about the little people they were responsible for? She'd seen it happen time after time. The people who were supposed to help the "lost children," as her foster mom had called them, didn't give a *damn*. They were there for the salary and the benefits a state job offered, not the welfare of the children.

Sam's constant wish was to somehow improve the system she'd grown up in after the death of her mom and sister. The only way change could happen was to work from the inside… to become a politician or a foster parent. Politics would *never* be something she was good at. Samantha didn't have a politically correct bone in her body. However, she could see herself as a foster parent, being a true advocate for children who grew up as she had. Of course, it would have to wait until she wasn't working thirty hours a day, six days a week.

"I know you do, sweetheart, but today we need to get your sick appendix out, so you feel better."

"Can't you just give me some medicine? I really don't want to have an operation."

Before Sam could answer, Miss Crutchfield's monotone voice sounded, causing Sam's fists to clench to keep from striking the woman. "Sydney, just do what the doctor says. Don't make trouble." And then the woman had the audacity to sigh.

Without a second thought, Sam reached across and grabbed the cell phone from the social worker's hands. When Miss Crutchfield looked up to complain, the woman's face lost all color. Sam could only imagine the expression she wore, but she was just too pissed off to give a shit. The woman was supposed to be *caring* for the sweet child, easing her fear at having surgery, being Sydney's support system. Not sitting there like a high school girl obsessed with her cell phone.

Samantha leaned down so they were eye to eye, and all but growled. "Miss Crutchfield, my name is Dr. Malone. Now, you can either be part of the solution or part of the problem. If you'd like to remain in this room, you'll need to be part of the solution. If you'd like to continue to completely ignore the child who needs your attention, then I suggest you go to the cafeteria and get a cup of coffee while we finish up Sydney's pre-op visit."

Miss Crutchfield's face immediately turned three shades of red. Without a word, she shot from her chair, took her phone from Sam's outstretched hand, and marched out of the room.

The cutest little giggle came from behind the young doctor and immediately calmed her temper. When she looked, Sydney had both of her pudgy little hands covering her mouth while her shoulders bounced with laughter. Just to see the child laughing, no matter how inappropriate, made all the frustration with the useless state employee worthwhile. At least the child wasn't in too much pain at the moment. It wouldn't do to have her suffering. Smiling while holding back her own laughter, Sam teased, "You think that was funny, do you?" Little blonde curls bounced as Sydney nodded. "Well, it was between two adults." Sam leveled her stare just a bit. "Always remember *your* manners."

"Yes, Dr. Sam," the child answered, still giggling.

Letting the subject drop, Sam moved on. "Okay, Miss Sydney, I'm going to show you exactly what will happen during your surgery and answer any questions you have. Then Dr. Schwartz will be in to give you some medicine that'll make you sleepy. Sound good?"

"Yes, ma'am." The child smiled, and all the long hours

seemed worth it just to know she could help people who truly needed it.

Once she finished her surgical residency, Sam wanted to be a general practitioner, with children and the elderly as the focus of her practice, no matter where she ended up. Charlie, officially known as Dr. Charlene Gallagher, had teased her from the moment they declared their specialties in med school. Her friend called it Sam's "opposite ends of the spectrum" focus. That wasn't the only ribbing she'd taken, but at least at school, Charlie had to bear it, too. Their classmates really had a blast with the fact that Sam and Charlie were roommates and best friends, "the girls with boys' names."

After about fifteen minutes of explaining, complete with a stuffed, cloth appendix, colored Expo markers, and a mini whiteboard, Sydney seemed utterly at ease. Sam stayed when the anesthesiologist came in. As her little patient started to yawn, she explained one more time, told the little sweetheart she'd see her in a few minutes, and headed to scrub up.

Hurrying down the hall, Sam remembered the way Sydney had smiled up at her, so trusting and loving. The sweet little girl's smile made all the long hours and millions of cups of coffee worth it. Affirmation that her decision to stay had been the right one came when she entered the Surgical Scrub Room and was confronted by Dr. Monoghan, along with the other three huge, male surgeons from his team. She knew she'd never be considered a "little girl." Sam was a tall, curvy girl and damn proud of it, but she felt almost dainty standing next to the behemoths scrubbing in with her.

Looking through the viewing window, she saw the doors across the vast expanse of the operating room open. In came one of her favorite orderlies, Adam, wheeling her young patient into the huge, instrument-filled room. Adam was the best with their pediatric patients, and rightfully so, since he and his wife were working on their own NBA team with three little boys under the age of six, their first baby girl on the way, and them already talking about more. Sam thought they were crazy, but they were good parents, and *that* was what was most important. Hurriedly, she put on her gown and gloves, then made her way to the operating room to reassure Sydney one last time before they started the countdown.

Sydney smiled up at her. "Hi, Dr. Sam," the little girl half-chuckled, half-slurred. She was responding well to the anesthesia. Some kids fought it and made the process horrible for all involved, but Little Blondie seemed to be able to adapt to almost anything life threw at her. Smiling down at the sweet child, Sam signaled to the anesthesiologist that he could begin. Time seemed to fly, and thankfully, everything went smoothly. In less than two hours, the young patient was being wheeled to the recovery room.

Samantha stayed with Sydney until the child was in her room and having the first of what the doctor was sure would be many red Jell-O cups. All the nurses loved the little girl on sight and laughed as she told everyone she only ate *red* Jell-O cups, none of the other "yucky" colors. As Sam was leaving, Sydney called out. "Dr. Sam, I didn't get a hug."

Choking past the lump in her throat, Samantha turned. "You're right. I'm sorry, sweetheart."

Walking the few steps back to the bed, Sam was immediately engulfed in the best hug she'd had in a long time. When she pulled back, Sydney was smiling from ear to ear. The resilience of children always seemed amazing to the doctor. Only a few hours ago, this sweet child had been in surgery, and now she was eating red Jell-O and hugging like a bear cub.

"Now, you be good, and I'll be back to check on you in the next day or two." She tweaked the little beauty's button nose.

"Yes, ma'am, Dr. Sam."

Sam was about halfway across the parking lot before she

realized her surgical cap was still on her head. As she pulled it off and shoved it in the large brown messenger bag she'd used since her freshman year in college, her long, thick, braid fell from under the cap and took its place in the center of her back. Laughing to herself, she realized her curly brown mane had been in a braid damn near every day since the first day of her internship almost seven years ago; even weirder was the comfort it gave her hanging against her back. At least her intricate design allowed her to keep the one thing she had in common with her mother *and* follow the rules of the hospital.

Leaving the hospital and the stress of a very long day farther behind with every step, she pulled the end of her braid to the front, removed the ponytail holder, and began unbraiding and finger-combing out the tangles as she went. As each of the strands separated, more of the tension from the last thirty hours also untangled and floated away. Somehow, letting her hair blow in the breeze was just what the doctor ordered. Sam knew by the time she reached her car it would be curling in every direction and she would resemble some wild child, fresh from the woods.

Breathing deeply, she inhaled and blew out all the anti-septic smells of the hospital. She finally had two days off *together* and doing whatever the hell she wanted for the next forty-eight...no, forty-two...hours was on the top of her list.

There was no regret about losing six hours of her off-time. Sydney was so worth it. It was Sam's job to help a child, and she'd do it again in a heartbeat. Hell, she might even sneak back tomorrow just to check on the child. After all, she *had* told the little darling she'd see her in the next day or two.

Sydney reminded her of all the kids she met when Fate saw fit for her to be in foster care. Sam had been one of the lucky ones. It had taken time, but she'd been placed with a great foster mom, and every day her tragedies from the past were a little easier to deal with. Too tired for a trip down memory lane, she focused on getting to her car.

Reaching into the pocket of her scrubs for her keys, the sensation of being watched raised the tiny hairs at the nape of her neck. Not in a creepy, stalker kind of way, but in a protected, almost special kind of way. As crazy as it seemed, Sam was filled with anticipation and excitement. It was reassuring to know *he* was watching over her.

The feeling of being watched had started after she'd been kidnapped from the very parking lot she now stood in and carried off to the middle of nowhere almost seven months ago. It had definitely been one of the most terrifying experiences of her life...one she would never forget, but not one she would let rule her life either. It was true she'd been fighting for her life that day, but there was no way in hell Sam would be a victim. Nothing, not even bad memories or bullies that preyed on women, could beat her. She still walked to her car by herself, politely avoiding the security guards she knew were told to watch out for her. It reminded her and others that she would *not* live in fear.

Everyone had her best interests at heart, she truly believed that. The hospital mandated psychiatrist recommended she get a roommate to avoid spending time alone after her abduction, but no way was going to happen. Memories of overcrowded rooms at full group homes, where she could feel the breath of the girl next to her while they slept, reminded Sam she needed her space.

The day she left Momma Maybelle's (the best foster mom in the world) for college, she'd promised herself "things" did not matter, but that she would have the privacy she'd so desperately needed for so many years. So, she'd worked long and hard, saved every penny she could, and two years ago had purchased her own home...a little oasis, away from everyone and everything, where she could sleep crossways on her bed until noon if she wanted.

Sam stopped dead in her tracks.

I sound like a spoiled brat.

Her next thought caused her to chuckle.

Okay, maybe I would share with someone.

The "someone" who came to mind was a big, muscular, hunk of a man with the most hypnotic eyes she'd ever seen, spiky blond hair, and a deep rumbling voice. She'd be willing to share so very many things with him.

Shaking her head in an attempt to restore what little sanity she had left, Sam continued walking, thinking more about how it was like she had a guardian angel...someone who watched over her kept her safe, protected her. She snorted out loud. "No, not an angel." The man who seemed to consume her thoughts more with every passing day could in no way be associated with the pink-cheeked little cherubs the word "angel" brought to mind. He was a Guardian, big and masculine and....*wow*.

Without a doubt, Sam knew it was him—the hottest man on the planet, with insurmountable strength, a power that seeped into her very bones the day they met, and a body that awakened dreams of hot, sweaty nights and incredible passion —who watched over her. He'd made her feel safe during one of the most terrifying ordeals of her life, and with the kind of life she'd lived since the fateful day all those years ago, that was really saying something.

Just his presence made her feel...no, made her know... everything was going to be all right—a totally new sensation for Samantha, one she couldn't remember ever feeling. He was different than any other man she'd ever met. It was hard to explain, even to herself. The best description she could come up with was that he was just...more. His touch infused her with warmth and security. It felt...right; not strange or foreign, but meant to be.

Sam knew he'd somehow helped her recover, and was a big part of why she'd gotten back to work so quickly. She was strong and had a determination to accomplish anything she put her mind to, but the trauma of that day had threatened her incredible resolve; and then, there he was. He'd lifted her from the rubble, and the missing pieces of her world had fallen into place. Parts she hadn't known were missing.

At least two of the other girls who were abducted at the same time were still in therapy. From time to time, Sam checked on them. They'd all been brought to her hospital... therefore, accessing their records and keeping track of them was simple. When her friend Charlie saw her reading their charts, she'd just smiled and walked away. Everyone knew how she felt about bullies, and as far as she was concerned, the scumbags who'd kidnapped them were the worst kind of bullies.

Sam prided herself on her inner strength, something she inherited from her father, or so she'd been told. It had rubbed her the wrong way when the hospital administration decreed she have six sessions with the hospital psychiatrist. She'd adamantly refused until they played hardball and refused to let her go back to work until the evaluation was complete. Doing the six sessions had been tedious and boring. She'd given all the right answers, and once it was finished, she was done.

There was no way in hell Sam was doing anymore, even though it was obvious Dr. Simons wanted her to. He often stopped by under the guise of checking on another patient or looking for the head of surgery, but she wasn't an idiot. It was apparent he was checking on her.

Not wanting to draw any more attention to the situation, Sam always smiled and gave the obligatory answers, while inside screaming to be left alone. Dr. Simons even resorted to asking about the cut on her leg when he could tell she was trying to get away. Donning her best smile, she'd tell him it had healed nicely with a minimum of scarring. Why wouldn't he realize there was no reason to rehash the gory details? It was over, she'd survived, and it was time to move on. That was how Dr. Samantha Malone dealt with things. Her continued prayer was that, sooner or later, the good doctor would find another "project" and leave her alone.

Thinking back to that dreadful night, most people would've relived the fear, but Samantha remembered what it had felt like to be lifted out of the rubble by *him*. If she concentrated hard enough, she could actually feel his arms around her. The way he'd moved the enormous pile of debris that had fallen on top of her after the explosion as if it weighed nothing, would be permanently carved into her memory.

The douche bags who'd grabbed her in the parking lot had obviously cut and run when the bombs went off. If it hadn't been for the two beams crisscrossing over her, Sam would've been crushed when the ceiling collapsed. She remembered struggling and cursing like a sailor on shore leave, trying to get out from under the heap. Suddenly there was daylight, and she was caught in the most unladylike position imaginable. Lying on her back, feet in the air, looking at the sexiest man to walk the earth, Sam was mortified.

Her first glimpse had been of those incredible eyes, the color of the forget-me-nots flowering in the garden behind the house she'd grown up in. So light a blue that in the sunlight they seemed almost colorless, but when they looked at her, they seemed to glow. It felt as if he reached inside and soothed her fears.

Despite his size, he'd been incredibly gentle. There was contained aggression emanating from his amazingly muscular arms as they wrapped around her. His primary focus was rescuing her, but he would seek vengeance on her behalf when she was safe. Samantha had been unable to speak, only feel, as he lifted her out of the prison the explosion had created.

When he'd spoken, the little bit of brain function she had left evaporated into thin air. The low rumbling of his voice wove its way under her skin and made her tingle. Since that day, she'd spent many lonely nights letting his whispered words of reassurance fuel her most erotic dreams. She always woke up wondering why he watched her but never approached.

Samantha couldn't explain, no matter how long she thought about it, how she knew without a doubt that he was a genuinely good guy. The word "hero" flashed in her mind like a neon sign and returned every time she thought of him, which happened to be too damned much. Her body and soul knew immediately he was safe...specifically safe for her.

The adrenaline that had kept her going throughout the entire ordeal bled from her body at the touch of his hand. All of her recognized him as someone she could trust, someone she could lean on, and that wasn't something Samantha Malone ever did. Her eyes slid shut as she remembered how her head lay against his chest of its own volition. She'd taken her first deep breath since the black bag had gone over her head and her back had hit the floor of the dark, windowless van she was thrown into.

Her rescuer continually asked if she was okay if she was hurt, even told her the cut on her leg didn't look too deep. She'd chuckled when he reassured her he was taking her to a "healer." By the time he laid her on a blanket under a tree far from the smoking building, the vibrations of his rich baritone voice had reached deep inside, relaxing her until she felt warm and calm.

At the loss of his warmth, her body ached...just another of the weird things she'd had to work through since that night. How could she feel anything after just a few minutes in his arms? Not to mention the shit she'd been through in those few horrible hours. Sam chalked it up to trauma and shock, but now, seven months later, she still thought about him and heard his strong, steady heartbeat echoing in her mind. She even imagined him walking through the halls of the hospital and dreamt about him night after night.

Entirely on autopilot, Sam unlocked the doors on her old blue Jetta and slid into the driver's seat. She'd thought about getting a new car a few times, but this one fit her like a glove. Besides that, she hated being in debt. Her house was enough for her to keep up with, at least while she was still in her residency. She just had to keep "Bonnie Blue" going for a couple more years. Leaning her head against the headrest, she took a deep breath, letting the stress of the day wash away.

Not surprisingly, as soon as her eyes slid shut crystal blue eyes were gazing back at her. Even in her imagination, she could feel him in the deepest corner of her soul. He was...she searched for the right description...just so much *more* than anyone she'd ever met before. "Larger than life" ...that was it! That described him to a tee.

Her mother had said the same thing about her father. Sam always wondered what it meant, but since meeting him, it had all become clear. She could hardly remember her dad...knew he'd been a brave soldier and died in battle, defending the country he loved, from the stories her mom told. He was a hero, medals and all, something she definitely associated with the sexy man who lifted her from her nightmares that day seven months ago.

Lance whispered through her mind. She'd been embarrassed when she'd had to ask the elderly woman who cleaned and bandaged her wounds the name of the man who'd carried her to safety. The healer said his name, and it was as if a breath of fresh air washed over her. It was like nothing she'd ever experienced.

Searching for answers, Sam decided it was a byproduct of all the adrenaline flooding her system. Of course, that didn't explain why she was sitting in her car after working an incredibly long shift thinking about him and smiling.

Damn that man!

What had he done to her? She laughed out loud at her own paranoia.

Like he has any control over you whatsoever.

It was all in her mind. She'd even looked up "Rescuer Syndrome" in her psychology textbooks and found she didn't have the symptoms or the personality for it. Figuring it might be her completely neglected libido crying out for help, she'd even entertained the thought of dating the cute new pharmacist who continued to ask her out, although she barely looked his direction and only grunted a few words here or there when he spoke.

The problem was, she didn't feel anything for him, even when he turned his hundred-watt smile and what others called incredible charm on her. It was hopeless. She was in lust with a man she'd seen for all of ten minutes, seven damn months ago, haunted by the idea of who she thought he was and unwilling to stop it.

Turning the key in the ignition and hoping the grinding sound she heard wasn't anything serious, Sam blasted Lady Gaga's "Applause," praying it would keep her awake on the thirty-minute drive home. Trying to decide whether she was more hungry or tired, she remembered there was nothing in her refrigerator even remotely edible and thought about stopping at the grocery store, but the longer she drove, the more exhaustion won out. Even a drive-thru sounded like too much work. Hopefully, the Pop-Tarts she'd gotten a few weeks ago hadn't turned to rocks in the cabinet, and with any luck, she'd be able to locate the single packets of Crystal Light in her junk drawer.

With the dilemma of food settled, she backed out of her parking spot, completely ignoring the extra little shake and shimmy Bonnie Blue made and headed towards the winding roads that would take her to her little haven in the woods.

READ ALL OF HAUNTED BY HER DRAGON

Get Your Copy!

Also Part of the Kindle Unlimited Library!

THE ONE THAT STARTED IT ALL!

Her Dragon To Slay,

Dragon Guard, Book 1

CHAPTER ONE

"Dammit, Grace, pick up the phone," she growled through gritted teeth at the third voicemail she'd had to listen to in the last five minutes.

"Everything okay, Kyndel?' Barney, the *nice* guy in her office, asked.

"Yeah, everything's fine. Just trying to find Grace."

"Oh! Anything I can help with?"

Kyndel thought about telling him her troubles, but Barney had been spending an excessive amount of time in her office lately. At first, she'd thought he was just being nice, but then he joined her hiking group, and just yesterday he showed up with her favorite no whip, nonfat, iced white chocolate mocha from the *frou-frou* coffee shop on the corner. It had been then Kyndel realized she was Barney's newest crush. It had been a long time between boyfriends and Barney was nice, but...um...*no*. As flattered as she was, there was no way she had an office romance.

'Don't shit where you eat' was one of the pieces of sage advice Granny had given her just after graduation. Not that it ever truly made sense to Kyndel, but she got the gist of it... keep your personal life *out* of the office.

She saw the puppy dog look on Barney's face and hated to crush his spirit, but Kyndel decided a brisk walk home would be better than leading the poor fellow on, in *any* way.

"No, but thank you so much." Then, to make sure he got the hint and skedaddled, she added, "Have a nice a weekend," before turning her chair and dialing Grace's office for the third time.

Voicemail *again*. Time to pack up and get the heck outta dodge before someone found something else for her to do. Bag on shoulder, scowl on face, and more than a little disgusted, Kyndel headed out of the office.

*Never loan Grace the car... Never loan Grace the car...*was the mantra playing on a loop in Kyndel's mind. She was madder than a wet hen and getting hotter by the minute. It was *no fun* to walk home after ten hours of work. *No fun* to be abandoned and forgotten by the best friend she'd loaned her car to. *No fun* to make the five-block journey past the park...in the dark.

At twenty-six, she rarely admitted her fear of the dark and held her aunts responsible for the phobia. Had they not made her watch 'The Brain Eaters' when she was only six years old, Kyndel was positive everything would've been just fine. It wasn't that she believed aliens would set loose a horde of parasites to eat every human brain on the planet; she had a *little* more sense than that. It was the feeling of being watched...like someone was hiding in the shadows, just waiting for an opportunity to scare the living daylights out of her. At the mere thought of her' phantom stalker', the hair stood up at the nape of her neck, and she walked a bit faster.

A sudden *thud,* and what sounded like footsteps pounding on the hard ground, had her stopping in her tracks. "What the...?" She gasped, opening her eyes wide, hoping it would help her see through the shadows.

Several tense seconds later—that felt like damn near forever—and Kyndel moved again. This time, her eyes slid side-to-side like the stupid black and white cat clock her granny used to have in the kitchen.

The farther she got from where she'd heard the 'thump,' the easier it was to convince herself it had just been kids sneaking into the park after hours. Manlove Park was a popular make-out spot for teenagers. There might've even been a time after moving to the city when Kyndel herself had been convinced to take a walk on the wild side, but that was a story for another day.

Shoot, now I wouldn't know the wild side if I tripped and fell in it.

It had been almost a year since she'd dated the muscle-headed jock from the gym. Three long, tortuous dates and all because he had an incredible body. Of course, dating the douche bag had come at a price. She'd spent the entire time listening to him drone on about his body parts...*and not the good ones*...and *only* when he wasn't checking out every other woman in the joint.

It wasn't that he'd hurt her feelings. Kyndel knew who she was and had never been under the misconception she would be Miss America. She had a few extra pounds, and her curves had curves, but she was cute and had a brain, something not everyone could claim. What had pissed her off the most about dating Vinnie was, she'd wasted three whole evenings of her life that she could never get back. The one compliment the jerk had given her had been about her skin; he thought it was beautiful. Her granny always called her complexion peaches and cream and said her freckles added character.

Yeah, cause I need more of that.

She sighed as she thought about how much of her youth

she'd wasted hating those tiny brown spots, until the day she realized they weren't going anywhere. It was time to buck up and learn to love them or stop looking in the mirror. From that day forward, she stopped using makeup to cover them and embraced her 'freckled-self.' She also learned to accept her curves. *If ya don't like 'em, don't look at 'em* was her motto. For the most part, she ate right and worked out at least three times a week. But dammit if she didn't love her Ben and Jerry's Cherry Garcia and someone would lose a hand if they tried to take it from her.

A loud *'thud'* echoed between the buildings. Kyndel stumbled to a stop. She looked and listened. The longer she thought about what she'd heard, the easier it was for her to convince herself someone had yelled for help. So, for the second time in about as many minutes, she searched the inky shadows for signs of life. Her anxiety level quadrupled the longer she stood still. She wanted to scream when only the sound of leaves rustling across the sidewalk and the occasional car passing by reached her ears.

Disgusted, she grumbled aloud, "You've gone bonkers, Kyn." The sound of her own voice somehow calmed her rankled nerves, and she added, "Get to stepping, girlie."

The clicking of her heels bounced off the brick wall of the library as she hurried past. Resuming her original mantra, she added *Must kill Grace* at the end for good measure.

"I swear when I get my hands on..."

Her words were cut short as the unmistakable sound of a man groaning came from the shadows.

A chill skittered down her spine.

Goosebumps covered her arms.

She counted to three, unable to move...simply listening... praying it was only her imagination. One deep breath later, she slid her right foot forward, prepared to make a beeline for home at a high rate of speed.

The groan came again. Closer than before. More desperate...almost pleading.

The need to help the injured grew within her. Turning towards the darkness, Kyndel searched for the source of the noise.

Shaking so much her teeth chattered, she looked for any sign of the man she *knew* needed her help.

"It's time to make a decision, Kyndel. Fight or flight. What's it gonna be? God knows, standing like a bump on a log isn't solving a *damn* thing."

Flight won. She turned, almost running, her satchel clutched tightly to her side like a lifeline.

"Keep your head up and eyes front. Home's only a few blocks away," she reassured herself, with the promise of snatching her best friend bald for the stupid mess she was in.

Feeling guilty and worried for Grace, her heart at war with her brain, Kyndel thought aloud, "Hope everything's okay..."

Grace had always been a little scatter-brained, but she'd never just *forgotten* Kyndel before. It bothered her that there'd been no answer at Grace's office or on her cellphone when Kyndel had tried to track her down before leaving the office. She'd even taken a chance and tried her own home because Grace had a key, but only got voicemail there, too. It was a war between anger and worry that accompanied most of her thoughts about her friend lately.

The running joke was that Grace spent most of her time hooking up with eligible bachelors she met at work. The good Lord *knew* her bestie was gorgeous; five foot nine, long raven hair, blue eyes, and a curvy body without an extra ounce of fat. To top it off, she was a first-year lawyer, with a promising career. Grace had it all...brains and beauty, the total package.

Giggling nervously, she gave herself a mental swat to the back of the head. She didn't want anything bad to happen to

Grace, just a bump or bruise, even a hangnail would explain being left. If she really had just forgotten, Kyndel was going to be *pissed* and more than a little hurt.

The shadows seemed to be closing in. Fear pushed Kyndel until she was almost jogging in her sensible work heels. Looking over her shoulder, the toe of her shoe caught an uneven piece of concrete, and from one heartbeat to the next, she was falling forward. Arms flailing, mouth stretched wide in a wordless scream, the sidewalk racing toward her face, everything around her seemed to happen in slow motion. All she could think was *that's gonna leave a mark*.

Bracing for impact, she squeezed her eyes tight and prayed...then nothing happened. Opening one eye, then the other, Kyndel found herself hanging above the sidewalk, looking at a pair of the biggest feet she had ever seen—and they were sexy.

Sexy feet? I really am losing it. Wait! Why the hell am I above the concrete?

Warmth radiated from the perfectly muscled arm wrapped around her midsection. Goosebumps emanated from the extra-large hand holding firmly to her blouse, just a little too close to her breast.

She wiggled to change position, the cushion of her well-rounded ass finding the ridges of an incredibly hard set of abs. She trembled. Her heart raced. Just the thought of the man that could hold her upright made up for all her previous mishaps.

Within just a few seconds, Kyndel's world turned on its axis. The scenery blurred as she was effortlessly spun around and immediately found herself sitting atop the body of her rescuer, looking at faded denim covering extremely muscular thighs. Laughing aloud, she asked herself, *wonder what part I'll see next?*

The same muscled arm that had saved her face from

inevitable demise now kept her upright. She did a one-eighty, draped her legs over his thighs, with her knees barely touching the sidewalk, and got her first look at the top half of her rescuer. All she could do was gape. He was absolutely the most handsome man she'd ever seen, with features that looked like they'd been carved by expert hands.

Even with his eyes closed, he gave off the distinctive air of authority. The dim light highlighted his high cheekbones and aristocratic nose, adding to the power she felt radiating from his every pore. His perfectly formed lips made visions of passionate kisses and hot, sweaty nights dance through her brain. It didn't help that all he had on was a pair of well-worn blue jeans.

She imagined that denim riding low on his tapered hips when he stood, highlighting the incredibly sexy dimples that sat on the front of his hips. She absolutely knew without looking they were there, and that simple bit of knowledge made her temperature rise another degree, despite the cool breeze.

At the touch of her fingertips against the cool skin of his neck, an electric current arced between them. Flashes of light burst before her eyes. She blinked to clear her vision, then felt for his pulse, strong and steady against her digit. Heat rose from his skin, making her worry he might have a fever. Her eyes wandered down his well-toned body. She scoffed, unsuccessfully trying to convince herself she was only checking for further injury.

Who the hell do you think you're fooling?

She continued her perusal, taking note of his massive shoulders and a chest that could've been sculpted from granite. The light smattering of hair that glistened in the shards of light from the streetlamps emphasized his nipples, which were pebbled from the cool breeze. Her mouth watered, and her pulse raced.

What the hell is it about this guy? Is he doused in pheromones? Or am I in heat?

Her eyes landed on the best set of abs she'd ever seen. Unable, or maybe it was unwilling, to stop her hand, she traced the defined lines of his eight-pack, mesmerized by the feel of his skin beneath her fingers. The electricity continued to flow between them. The sound of a horn in the distance pulled her from her musing and brought her current situation into the glaring light of reality. The sexy man that had kept her from breaking her face on the concrete was out cold, and she was paying him back by sitting on his lap and copping a feel.

She scrambled to her feet, surprised her rescuer hadn't moved an inch during her less than graceful attempt to remove her butt from his lap. But there he lay, unmoving, except for the rise and fall of his chest. The longer he remained unconscious, the more panicked she became.

Looking up and down the street and cursing Grace for the hundredth time, Kyndel wished for her car. First Aid class had taught her *never* to move an injured person unless you knew what was wrong. Not that she could pick him up and carry him, anyway. The dude was *HUGE*. At least six-foot-three or four, and his muscles had muscles. She prayed he hadn't hit his head on the sidewalk. A concussion could be really bad if not treated.

"You're worried about a concussion now?" She scolded herself. "You've been drooling over the guy while his head is lying on the cold, hard sidewalk. Brilliant, Kyn, just brilliant." Reaching for her satchel, she grabbed her old sorority sweatshirt from inside, wadded it up, and knelt forward to lift his head.

Her fingers tangled in his soft, brown hair. The scattered shards of light made it look like melted chocolate flowing over her skin.

Would it shine in the sun or maybe have highlights? Some lighter brown mixed with red, even a few blond streaks woven throughout?

The silky softness of his tresses turned to something wet and sticky.

Blood!

Kyndel gulped. Panic seized the breath in her lungs as the true severity of the situation smacked her in the face. She fought to keep her calm. Now, there was absolutely no denying he needed medical attention. Reaching into her bag and cursing herself for not thinking of it sooner, she dug around for her cellphone.

Coming up empty-handed, she instantly remembered plugging it into her car charger the night before, not giving it the slightest thought until that moment. Cursing and threatening death to anyone in the immediate vicinity, she sat back on her heels and thought.

All I know to do is run down the street for help.

Looking at the fallen man, then in the direction of the Mini Mart, she reasoned he'd probably be okay. She'd be gone five minutes...*tops*. Run in, use the phone, run back. It all seemed very logical, but fear something would happen to him in her absence kept her in place.

This guy was important to her. That alone had all her red flags flying and bells and whistles screaming in her brain. She tried to push her feelings aside and look at the situation with logic, but that was like holding back a freight train with her pinky finger...*not gonna happen*. Besides, her granny would most definitely haunt her and probably kick her butt if she turned her back on someone who needed help.

"No one's gonna mess with this behemoth, even if he *is* unconscious," she reassured herself. "He probably doesn't have a wallet to steal anyway."

Should she dig in his pockets to try to find one? Some kind of ID?

Nah.

She wasn't keen on trying to explain her hand in his pants if he woke up. Her cheeks warmed at the thought of touching him again.

"What are you doing out at night in just a pair of jeans and bare feet, anyway?" she asked the unconscious man. "Guess it doesn't matter. You need help, whether you're dressed properly or not."

Hooking her satchel over her shoulder, Kyndel stood and took one last look at her 'patient.' Before she had barely moved an inch, a large, warm hand latched onto her bare ankle.

"What the hell?" she screamed, trying to pull her leg free while looking down to see what new fresh hell had befallen her.

READ THE WHOLE STORY HERE!

IT'S FREE!

ABOUT JULIA

Hey, Y'all! Julia Mills, the Sassy Southern Storyteller here. Thanks so much for stopping by. Hope all is well with you and yours. In my world, a good book where a Vivacious Heroine beats the odds and gets her hot Alpha will never let you down. I freely admit, I'm kinda partial to guys with scales and wings, but hey, I can love a Hero with fangs and fur just as much!

I LOVE stalkers! Facebook! Instagram! Hop on over and follow me on BookBub or Amazon. You can even sign up for my newsletter right here. And my website is www.JuliaMills-Author.com. (Wow! I'm everywhere! LOL!)

Take Care of YOU and ALWAYS Dare to Dream!

Talk to ya' soon!

XOXO Julia

ALSO BY JULIA MILLS

Find Them All on Amazon

The Dragon Guard Series

DRAGON GUARD BERSERKERS
Banning

ASHER
RAYNOR

Ladies of the Sky
Sadie's Shadow

Southern Fried Sass Series
Later Gator
Nosey Rosie
Lazy Daisy

THE 'NOT-QUITE' LOVE STORY SERIES
Vidalia: A 'Not-Quite Vampire Love Story

Phoebe" A 'Not-Quite' Phoenix Love Story
Zoey: A 'Not-Quite' Zombie Love Story
Jax: A 'Not-Quite' Puma Love Story
Heidi: A 'Not-Quite' Hellhound Love Story (Magic &
Mayhem Kindle World)
Lola: A 'Not-Quite' Witchy Love Story (Magic & Mayhem
Kindle World)
Sammie Jo: A 'Not-Quite' Shifting Witchy Love Story (Magic
& Mayhem Kindle World)
Harmony: A 'Not-Quite' Haunted Love Story (Magic &
Mayhem Kindle World)

KINGS OF THE BLOOD

VIKTOR: Heart of Her King ~ Kings of the Blood ~ Book 1

ROMAN: Fury of Her King - Kings of the Blood - Book2
ACHILLES: Soul of Her King - Kings of the Blood - Book 3

CAUGHT: A Vampire Blood Courtesan Romance
CONDEMNED: A Vampire Blood Courtesan Romance

MARROK: A Wolf's Hunger

Out of the Ashes: Guardians of the Zodiac: Pisces - Book 1
Scorched Ember: Guardians of the Zodiac: Taurus - Book 2

Alaric: A Vampire's Thirst

Printed in Great Britain
by Amazon

46223730R00145